MW01680926

BOON & EARL RAY

POO-DUNK LIFE

GEORGE GILLETTE

ISBN:
Paperback: 979-8-950932-16-8
Hardback: 979-8-950932-17-5

Published by North Bridge Publishers

Printed in the United States of America

ACKNOWLEDGMENTS

As always, my deepest love and endless gratitude go to the love of my life, my rock and greatest supporter — my wife, Delia. Without her constant encouragement, patience, and belief in me, this book would never have seen the light of day.

I also want to dedicate this book to my dear Redneck friend, Paul Minter, who is now fishing in the rainbows of heaven. Paul, your wild spirit, your laughter, and your friendship meant more to me than words can ever say. I miss you every single day, brother. This one's for you.

A special thank you goes to Christian Mendez of Northbridge Publishing for his unwavering support, guidance, and belief in this project. Your help has been invaluable.

Finally, I want to express my heartfelt appreciation to St. Jude Children's Research Hospital. A portion of the profits from the sales of this book and others will be donated to this extraordinary institution. Walking through the halls of St. Jude, seeing the courage of those brave children and the tireless dedication of the doctors, nurses, and staff, reminds me of what truly matters. They give hope and healing to families facing the unimaginable, and they do it with compassion, science, and love. Knowing that some of the proceeds from these pages will help continue their life-saving mission fills my heart with purpose and joy. Thank you, St. Jude, for everything you do.

About the Book

Welcome to Poo-Dunk County, Georgia. Where the sweet tea is strong, the duct tape is stronger, and common sense is strictly optional.

Meet Boon and Earl Ray: two good ol' boys whose combined brainpower usually hovers somewhere between "mildly dangerous" and "hold my beer." From battling a talking plastic box they call "Al-e-x-a," to turning a toaster into a flaming Pop-Tart catapult, then there is the mud-bog wedding and glitter-bomb revenge schemes; these fellas turn everyday life into pure comedy of gold.

Whether they're inventing a chest-freezer air conditioner, chasing ghost fishermen, surviving the world's worst water-ski launch, or debating the proper way to tip a self-checkout machine, Boon and Earl Ray prove one thing: in the South, the best stories aren't the ones that go right. They're the ones that go gloriously, hilariously wrong, especially when someone yells. "Watch this."

You will find enough Southern charm to make a possum grin. Boon and Earl Ray is a love letter to country living, backyard ingenuity, and the simple. If you've ever fixed something with baling wire and prayer, laughed until beer came out of your nose. Believe life is better when it's a little muddy, then pull up a porch chair, crack open a cold one, and get ready. Because in Poo-Dunk County, every day is another adventure.

About the Author

George Gillette is a proud man through and through. A devoted husband and father of five, he's spent most of his life in the Peach State, where the sweet tea flows freely, and the backroads never run straight. When he's not writing tall tales from Poo-Dunk County, you'll find him deep in the woods hunting, on a quiet creek bank fishing, swapping stories with friends, or just soaking up outdoors, like a cat in the sun.

George firmly believes that life is better when you're laughing, that duct tape can fix almost anything (except maybe a marriage and stupid). The best stories start with someone, "This is no lie." He pours all that country heart, hard-earned wisdom, and redneck ingenuity into every story he tells. This is because in his world, every mishap is just another laugh in the making.

INTRODUCTION:

DUCT TAPE, DUMB LUCK & POO-DUNK MAYHEM

Welcome to Poo-Dunk County, Georgia, where the stories are taller than a pine tree, and common sense takes a permanent vacation the second somebody hollers, "Hey y'all, watch this!"

If you've ever wondered what happens when two good ol' boys with more imagination than sense, a cooler full of beer, and a garage full of duct tape get turned loose on everyday life, then pull up a lawn chair, crack open something cold, and settle in. This book is a love letter to the glorious mess that is life in the holler.

Meet Boon and Earl (sometimes called Earl Ray when he's really in trouble). They ain't heroes, and they're barely even role models. What they are is a walking, talking, beer-swilling comedy show that proves one eternal truth: nothing ever goes according to plan, but it usually makes one hell of a story.

Inside these pages, you'll find chili so hot it needs its own fire department, turkey hunts that end in friendly fire, raccoon rodeos, glitter-bombed revenge, homemade air conditioners that attract wildlife buffets, and enough questionable decisions to fill a county jail on a Saturday night. You'll witness mud-bog weddings, Dollar General riots, a potential alien abduction, and the sacred gospel of "Hold my beer."

This ain't fancy literature. It's just pure, unfiltered chaos served with a side of fried okra and a healthy dose of "bless their hearts." These stories celebrate the kind of people who fix problems with baling wire, turn disasters into legends, and understand that the best memories are made when everything goes spectacularly wrong.

So, ignore the ringing in your ears from that last bottle-rocket rodeo, and come on in.

Y'all enjoy yourselves now.

And whatever you do—don't try this at home.

TABLE OF CONTENTS

Chapter One:

Boon and Earl vs. Al-ex-a Fancy Talkin' Box

Boon lives way back in the foothills, where the GPS signal dies and the roads are mostly just “that way.” Go past the big rock that looks like a busted fridge, and that's where their houses sit. His best friend and partner, Earl Ray, lives right next door—which in these parts means a half-mile down a dirt path that turns into a rushing creek every time it rains.

Boon’s yard isn’t so much a yard as it is a glorious mess of rusted-out appliances, half-buried in weeds like modern art nobody asked for. There are nine rusty trucks in various stages of “we swear we’ll fix ‘er up someday,” currently serving as luxury chicken condos. The chickens run around like they own the place, which they basically do. They’ve got more square footage than Boon’s actual house.

Wandering through this glorious chaos are two fat, deeply judgmental pigs who think they’re German Shepherds. They roam freely with the goats, who have formed an unholy alliance of absolute destruction. The goats eat everything that isn’t nailed down, including Boon’s one good work boot.

Meanwhile, the turkeys and geese sit in their wire pen like grumpy old men on a porch, silently judging everyone. The head turkey, especially, has a murderous temper and has been known to chase Earl Ray across the property for sport.

Boon and Earl Ray are simple, beautiful creatures that technology forgot. Honestly, technology is probably relieved. These boys still think Wi-Fi is an infectious disease, something you catch if you stand too close to the microwave. We once spent twenty minutes watching them try to plug a router into a wall socket, "so the internet would come out warmer."

Earl Ray once proudly held up a glowing modem and said, "Boon, this little feller puts out some good heat. We oughta take 'er inside when it gets cold."

Boon nodded wisely and replied, "Long as it don't start talkin' like that Alexa woman. I don't need no robot lady judgin' my grocery list."

They're not stupid. They're just... well, selectively advanced. They can rebuild a 1978 Chevy engine with a coat hanger, a flathead screwdriver, a crescent hammer, and pure elbow grease. But ask them to send a text message, and they'll look at you like you just asked them to perform brain surgery on a rabid squirrel. God bless 'em. They're happy and living life exactly how they want.

Their collective IQ isn't so much a high number as a daily temperature reading. The score is a variable that fluctuates wildly depending on the nearest distraction, rumored to be a two-digit figure requiring a decimal point. It's said it sits somewhere between the price of a small bag of corn chips and the number of times Earl has locked his keys in his truck while it was still running. Look out—their intelligence should probably come with a bright yellow hazard warning sign.

They believe "the Cloud" is a literal place where it rains, and they wait for it to download the weekly weather. Their most complex thought process is usually limited to debating about original corn chips, cheap beer, and women. Their absolute pinnacle of technology is an electric can opener that still works on the first try. For sure, they will never forget the simple things, because they've never truly grasped the complicated ones. They live with the idea that the best way to handle the future is to look backward. It's perfect proof that sometimes, a complete lack of sophistication is the most authentically human thing of all!

Today, Boon plugged in a sleek device, which he insisted was made in a "space-age government lab." Earl approached it cautiously, holding a rusty wrench like it might bite.

"Now, how does this thing work, Boon?" Earl whispered. "Why ain't it got a rabbit-ear antenna?"

Boon grinned. "This here thing I got from Willy the tire guy," he explained, tapping the top of the device. "He said it's an Artificial Smartness thing, Earl. It listens and talks. My nephew said you gotta talk nicely to it, like you're talking to a prize hound dog or that sweet gal who serves the taters at the church social. Now go on, say 'Hey Al-e-x-a,' and ask about the weather, and it will tell you everything."

Earl cleared his throat and addressed the device with exaggerated politeness. "Excuse me, Box. Ma'am? We need to know about the weather and if the crappies are biting."

Silence.

"You gotta say the wake-up word, Earl. Willy explained the instructions after he hooked it up. Just say, 'Al-e-x-a,' then ask a question!"

Earl looked deeply offended. "Al-e-x-a? It's a Box! We can't just go naming factory products. There are laws against that! That's how you void the factory warranty and return policies!"

The box suddenly made a sharp ringing sound.

Earl sighed. "Fine. Hey, Al-e-x-a, Box! Wake up!"

A voice answered, calm and clear: "I am awake and ready."

Earl gasped, dropping his wrench. "It talks! Al-e-x-a Box, listen up. We're looking forward to knowing if it will rain tomorrow. Are the fish biting? Don't you lie to us, because we already got the lawn chairs and fish rods out. Al-e-x-a, what's the weather tomorrow?"

"The forecast for tomorrow in Poo-Dunk, Georgia, is clear skies with a high of 75 degrees," the calm voice replied.

Earl was amazed, then leaned in so close to the box his nose was touching the plastic. "Wait a minute. Seventy-five degrees? That ain't no damn fish report! Al-e-x-a Box! You don't know nothin' 'bout fishing! Al-e-x-a, you're just repeating what the local weatherman said yesterday, ain't ya?"

It answered, "I am accessing and synthesizing data from meteorological services."

Earl squinted at the machine. "Synthesizing? See, Boon, it's making crap up! It's just a fancy liar in a plastic box! Boon, you know, if we want to know the weather, we look at the sky. If the sky doesn't tell us, we wait until we get wet!"

With that, Earl declared, "That Box needs to be unplugged immediately. Artificial Intelligence stuff doesn't hold a candle to a good, old-fashioned cloud lookin'. If my big toe hurts, it will rain."

They both agreed and pulled the plug on the thing. "You're fired, Al-e-x-a," Boon muttered. Then he looked at the cord dangling from his hand. “Well, now what do we do with this thing? It has a good three feet of useful copper wire.”

Earl, ever the pragmatist with low standards, immediately lit up. “Wait a minute. It's round, it's plastic, and it makes a rattling noise when you shake it. It might be a cat toy!” He tossed the high-tech device onto the floor for the nearest bewildered tabby cat.

The cat ignored it completely and instead rubbed happily against a rusty tin can near the trash.

“See, Boon?” Earl said. “Even a barn cat knows that simple things are best! That cat can synthesize as well as that box!”

And so, the age of sophisticated gadgetry ended right then and there. It was less effective than a replacement fishing lure.

Chapter Two:

Hold My Sweet Tea

Buckle up, y'all! 'Cause Ol' Hillbilly Boon's revving his rusty pickup, and he's got a serious hankerin' to spill the beans on them hidden highways that turn a plain ol' drive into a wild whoop-de-doo!

Yup, Boon's your trusty sidekick: a weathered fella with a rig that's seen more miles than a migrating goose. He has a jug of "revvin' elixir," and smarts so rustic they'll have your overalls dancin' the jig. Boon's the type who charts courses by the aroma of fried chicken and has a solid, deep-seated skepticism of fancy GPS gadgets. His down-home tips on prime country lanes are dished out with a side of laughs plainer than a dirt road after a heavy rain. Now, let's kick up some dust and burn some miles!

Boon was driving on a highway and then suddenly veered off like he was evading a swarm of angry bees, steering toward a wiggly strip of asphalt that seemed laid by tipsy beavers.

He turned to Earl in the passenger seat, who was hanging halfway out the window.

"Highways?" Boon grunted, flicking boiled peanut shells out of the cab windows. "Freeways are for fancy folks hurryin' to corporate meetings. The prime country lanes are where America's soul is tucked away. Them roads are curvin' like a snake in a hurry and jostling a butt fiercer than a rodeo bronc. We once cruised one in Georgia that looped up and was so wild, I swore we waved at our own taillights. Landed right in a peach cobbler fest where the fruit was so ripe, it practically peeled itself. Earl, that Georgia Peach moonshine will make a fella love a fat gal quick as a canebrake rattler!"

He scooted a little closer to the steering wheel, his grin sparklin' like stars over a campfire. He talked to the cracked bobblehead dogs on the dashboard and to Earl, who was busy opening his next beer.

"Now listen up, partner: life's too short to be drivin' the boring straightaways. The real lessons live out on these twisty country lanes. Teaches patience, teaches character. Kinda like waitin' for Auntie Mina's sweet pies to cool or watchin' thick bacon fry in a cast-iron skillet.

You gotta mind the hazards on these old dirt roads, though. There are potholes big enough to swallow a pickup truck whole. Round these parts, we call 'em City Slicker Snares. Then you got the road hogs—actual, literal hogs—laid out in the middle of the asphalt like they booked the place for a hotel. And those signs sayin' 'Dead End'? Don't you believe it for a second. That sign just means the adventure starts here. Just yell, 'Hold my beer, strap that seat belt on,' and we will make a new road right through the brush."

Boon took a long swallow of beer and continued. "Why, just last month, we hit a road that squeezed down to one lonely dirt track. Ran right into a fella drivin' a massive hay baler comin' the other way. There wasn't room for both of us, so we had to settle it with rock-paper-scissors for the right of way. We lost. Had to back up almost a whole mile in reverse." Boon guffawed, pounding the dashboard with his fist.

"There's critters round these parts, too. Squirrels dart out like they're late for nut school, and if ya dodge too much, it's ditch-bathing time. Hot tip: Spot a possum amblin' across the yellow line? Give it the gas! That roadkill possum pot roast and gravy ain't half bad if you season it right."

"Another piece of advice from us: Don't smoke them left-handed cigarettes. They will make you eat like a prize pig and giggle like a goose for four hours straight. Another thing to remember, Earl, is to keep them secret fishing spots chillier than a well-digger's boots. Remember, tell one, tell all. Now pass me a beer."

Earl crawled out the broken back window of the cab, opened the cooler in the truck bed, and grabbed two cold beers. He climbed back in and handed one to Boon.

Boon continued, swerving around a stump. “Good thing we got neighbors so warm they'll rope ya into a backyard barbecue even if ya show up lookin' like you tangled with a wild thorn bush. But steer clear of the 'quick route' that takes an extra four hours by Googling with those fancy cell phones. Look around in the woods, and you will find the universe tellin' ya to ease up and sniff the wildflowers. Last piece of advice is if you get so drunk that you're seeing double, just drive with one eye closed. Works every time at the sobriety checkpoints.”

Earl Ray stuttered, looking into the plastic bin, “He-He-Hey. We are completely out of beer.”

Boon immediately slammed the truck into four-wheel drive, spun a donut in the dirt, and headed straight for home.

Chapter Three:

The Cork Dances and the Stereo Plays Itself

Earl leaned forward at a crackling campfire deep in the woods. The firelight flicked across his grizzled face like he was about to drop the ancient secret to eternal life, or at least the absolute best live bait for catching crappies. He cleared his throat, spat a stream into the flames (which hissed back violently), and launched into a slow Southern drawl that could stretch a short story into a three-day holiday weekend.

"This here is no lie. A long time ago, back when my hair still knew what color it was supposed to be and was growin' long in my ears—back when I didn't scare small children just lookin' at them—well now, we're driving through an abandoned mill town down in Mississippi. The place was so dead that even the weeds had given up on it and gone to Florida for the winter. The town had boarded-up windows and rusted silos leanin' over like town drunks at last call. There was not one single living soul around 'cept for the giant mosquitoes and us.

The Jeep was running dangerously low on gas, and the paper map was entirely useless. Then the radio started laughin' at us in Mandarin Chinese. Well, we just kept drivin' till the odometer started spinnin' like a broken Mexican slot machine on a heavy bender. Next thing we know, we stop over by this old mill pond that's half-choked with green lily pads and deep regret.

There's this strange fella sittin' on a rotting stump fishin'. He’s got a bamboo rod in one hand and an old can of worms in the other. Tall, skinny, wearin' overalls older than dirt and a ball cap so faded it just had the letter 'B' on it. We think it should have said 'Been Here Since Before Electricity.' We figured he was just another lost tourist, so we hollered, 'Hey, buddy, you know the way out of here?'

He turned around slowly, grinned with teeth that looked like they lost a physical fight with a piano, and said real calm, 'Son, civilization left this town back in '47. People took the jobs, the jukebox, and the best fishin' spots right along with them.'

The place went dead quiet. Then this man says, ‘Hey, I got some advice fer you.’

Well, shoot, we ain't ones to turn down free stuff, so we sat down in the dirt and listened. Turns out he's got secrets that'd make a largemouth bass blush—not saying what they were in mixed company, of course. He tells us to use nightcrawlers with tinfoil at dusk. Says to only use the ones that wiggle counterclockwise. Says it's 'respectful to the current.' He swears a crankbait painted John Deere green catches twice as many fish when you hum 'Sweet Home Alabama' and hold your mouth open like a channel catfish. We were takin' notes like he was the second comin' of Jesus H. Walton.

Then he starts gettin' really philosophical on us. Well, that ghost looks right at Earl and says, 'Earl'—because we're on a first-name basis now—'I forgot to clock out or can't find the right door. Do you know where the grave and the path out is?' Well, we're nodding along like we understand the mystery, but inside we're thinkin', 'Wait, bet this old spook knows exactly where the hidden moonshine still is.'

Before we can even ask, the broken stereo in the Jeep—which had been completely dead for three states—suddenly crackles to life and blasts the twangiest honky-tonk music you've ever heard in your life. George Jones is wailin' about cryin' time, and the mechanical odometer starts goin' completely berserk, spinnin' backwards like it's tryin' to un-drive us outta that county.

Then that ghost stands right up, tips his ancient ball cap, and starts doin' the most ridiculous line dance we've ever seen. His arms are flappin' like a wild chicken on a fresh shot of espresso. His work boots are kickin' up clouds of dust that literally glow in the moonlight. He's two-steppin', grapevinin', and even throws in a little Macarena for flair. The fishin' pole is still in his hand, and that cork bobber is bouncin' in the air like it's keepin' perfect time with the music.

We blink once—poof. He's completely gone. No footsteps left in the mud, no goodbye, just the faint echo of a final 'Yee-yaw!' ringin' through the trees. Our radio cuts out mid-chorus like somebody yanked the battery cable. The place is dead quiet again. The odometer snaps right back to normal. The only crazy thing left is that Earl's phone has a new text message note that reads: 'Counterclockwise worms. Hum Sweet Home Alabama, and smile like a catfish.'

So yeah, boys and girls. Spooks got good yarns to spin. And killer footwork too. Moral of the story? Next time you're lost in a ghost town, look for some fresh bait... and maybe some dancin' shoes. You never know when a ghost will go Boot Scootin'."

Earl sat back from the campfire, took a long pull from his twelfth beer, and grinned like a man who'd just won a high-stakes bet with the afterlife. The fire popped loudly. Somebody in the shadows chuckled.

Then he added, "Prime country lanes ain't mere routes; they're sassy stand-offs against the everyday grind. Cherish the heavy jolts, chuckle at the weird sidetracks, and don't forget: if yer truck fenders ain't speckled with mud, grit, and fresh bird crap, yer missin' out on some good times. Stow an extra fan belt in the cab, and perhaps a harmonica for the tough spots. 'Cause on a country lane, every single mix-up's just a tall tale in the makin'!"

Chapter Four:

Duct Tape Diplomacy and Turkey Hunter Warnings

Y'all listen up, because this here's the real deal from Poo-Dunk. The true soul of Poo-Dunk County ain't nowhere near no courthouse or no fancy book-learnin' place (supposin' Poo-Dunk ever paid for one). Nah, you gotta find it right on Boon’s porch where that screen door squeaks louder than a dyin' chicken, and mostly the way folks talk is with a thoughtful grunt and a good ol' fart after dinner.

Boon and Earl ain't just folks; they're the danged pioneers of genuine, unvarnished Poo-Dunk livin'. They are the ultimate fashion statement ‘round here: Boon wears about 90% overalls and 10% flannel most times, all 100% permanently stained with something mysterious like motor oil, soppin' gravy, or tobacco juice. Earl ain't bought a new ball cap since '66. The one he wears is only holdin' up thanks to dried sweat salt, duct tape, and sheer, stubborn dirt.

Their rides ain't about gettin' from here to there; they're about maintainin' a legacy of highly questionable vehicular engineering. Boon's truck is lifted so high he needs a literal step ladder just to climb into the cab, and the radio only plays country music from artists who have been in jail at least twice.

Earl's souped-up golf cart has official road tags, makin' it legally Poo-Dunk's fastest vehicle on the highway. That mechanical monstrosity can hit 90 miles an hour when it's rollin', usually after Earl has downed a jar of moonshine and poured whatever was left directly into the gas tank.

They're certified experts in the three main Southern food groups: stuff you can eat out of a can, stuff you can slap on a Ritz cracker, and stuff you can drop into a bubbling oil fryer. Their favorite dinner is a delicacy they call "Roadkill Surprise." They named it that because it's always a genuine surprise what the hounds happen to drag in from the yellow line of Highway 12.

Around here, security ain't about cameras, alarms, or monthly subscriptions. It's about pure, old-fashioned deterrence. The kind that makes a fella think twice before steppin' foot where he don't belong. It's all about scarin' folks off before they even get started.

Boon's got a big ol' handmade wooden sign nailed right to his front porch post, the letters burned deep into the oak with a red-hot fireplace poker so they'll never fade. It reads:

"Trespassers will be shot. Survivors will be shot again. All the rest, not buried and still bleeding, will be put in jail if they survive the drag behind the truck getting them into town."

To make sure nobody thinks it's a joke, he keeps an old rusty single-barrel 12-gauge leaned right up next to the front door so visitors can see he ain't bluffin'. Folks say he ain't had a single theft in forty years. Even the Jehovah's Witnesses just wave nervously from the safety of the road now. To be fair, no one wants to steal the old cracked toilets, broken washing machines, and dead refrigerators cluttering up the front yard anyway.

Then there's Earl and his prize hound named Six-Toe Dawg. The dog ain't mean—he's actually pretty friendly once your eyes stop watering from the smell. But Lord help you if you cross that property line after dark. Six-Toe is a tactical genius when it comes to biological warfare.

He patrols the perimeter every night and leaves highly effective, stinky landmines all along the fence line, the driveway, and especially right around the tool shed. We're talkin' fresh, squishy, eye-watering deposits that smell like something crawled up a bloated possum's backside and died of old age. Step in one of them masterpieces, and you'll be trackin' that aroma into next Tuesday.

Earl just chuckles, cracking open a cold one, and says, “Boy, that dog ain't just security... he's a one-dog early warning system. If the smell don't stop 'em, the tracking will.”

Between Boon's sign and Six-Toe's special daily gifts, their places stay safer than most folks' houses with all those electronic gadgets. Because at the end of the day, ain't no motion sensor or fancy doorbell camera that hits quite like the fear of gettin' shot twice or steppin' into the absolute abyss of Six-Toe's digestive track. It's country home security: cheap, effective, and deeply memorable.

These boys reckon duct tape is the end-all, be-all problem solver and the greatest emergency repair tool ever gifted to mankind. If a problem can't be fixed with duct tape, gorilla glue, a shotgun, or a bit of fishing line, then it simply can’t be fixed.

Their philosophy for handling life's obstacles is simple: laugh at it, shoot it, ignore it, or throw it out into the yard. If you go to the grocery store, don’t worry about reading the ingredients on the back. If the can says tomatoes, that’s what's in there—and if it ain't, the frying pan will fix it anyway.

Everything must be perfectly balanced in life. That’s why Boon and Earl make sure to always hold a beer in each hand, maintaining perfect physical equilibrium at all times.

CHAPTER FIVE:

THERMO-DEE-NAMICS OR THE GREAT POP-TART APOCALYPSE

The day kicked off as most great Poo-Dunk engineering projects do: with a simple, desperate need and a zero-dollar budget.

Boon's ancient toaster oven had developed a serious personality disorder. It was only browning one side of his main culinary delicacy, Cherry Pop-Tarts, leaving the other side pale, cold, and sad like a tourist who forgot his sunscreen at the public creek.

"She's got uneven heat, Earl," Boon declared, looking at the appliance like it had personally insulted his ancestral lineage. "We have got a clear case of failure of thermo-dee-namics here."

Earl poked at the heating element with a chewed-up toothpick he'd been using as a dental tool for the last three days. "Looks like a busted spring to me."

Instead of doing the responsible thing and spending a whole twenty bucks on a brand-new toaster at the Dollar

General, they decided to "tune 'er up" like it was a '62 Chevy with a bad carburetor and a blown gasket.

First step: get supplies. They dug up some scrap rubber, a wire coat hanger, three rolls of duct tape, and a crescent wrench that doubled as a hammer. They opened a jar of pickled eggs they'd been saving for "national emergencies," and cracked open a fresh case of warm beer to fuel the operation. Nothing says precision engineering quite like a blood alcohol level that could pickle a wild hog and blow up a police breathalyzer.

Boon took the oven apart using a rusty butter knife in one hand and a pair of pliers he usually saved for pulling teeth—either his own, the dog's, or the neighbors', depending on who had the active toothache. Within seconds, three tiny, vital screws rolled off the porch and disappeared into the weeds forever, never to be seen again.

To get more spring tension on the door mechanism, Earl made a scientific-mechanical decision. "We need us some counter-weightin'," he announced in his best fake university professor voice. He ran off into the yard and came back with a smooth, heavy river rock. "That there'll hold the heat down and balance the tension. It's physics, Boon. Pure physics," he said, slamming his fourth beer.

For the final touch, because every Poo-Dunk masterpiece needs that one inspired, bizarre flourish, Boon replaced the long-missing temperature knob with a solid brass valve handle he ripped off a busted bathtub rotting in the woods. "Feels sturdy," he muttered, giving it a proud, heavy twist.

Then came the moment of ultimate glory. "Hold the coat hanger and this rubber gizmo in place, Earl," Boon ordered. He slapped twenty feet of heavy-duty black duct tape around the contraption, wrapping the entire outside of the oven until it looked like a black, mummified football with rogue copper wires sticking out of the top.

They plugged it into an ungrounded extension cord. The toaster oven immediately let out a terrifying sound like a big ol' swarm of mad hornets that had just drank five cans of energy drinks and ate two pounds of pure sugar. The toaster started shaking violently on the table, followed by a deeply worrying pattern of hum… pop… hum… bang... crackle.

"Hear that, Earl?" Boon beamed, proud as a new daddy, swallowing down his sixth beer. "That's power! We done fixed her up!"

With all the unearned confidence of two men who had never met a consequence they couldn't outrun, they cranked the brass bathtub valve all the way to the 'MAX' setting.

Here's what happened next:

That heavy-duty rubber band—which was actually a thick slice Earl had hacked out of an old tractor tire inner tube—

had been stretched tighter than a politician's promise on election night. It sizzled from the intense heat, melted through the wire hanger, and then snapped with a noise like a 12-gauge shotgun going off inside a phone booth.

The river rock, having reached critical thermal mass inside the taped-up chamber, turned the toaster into a makeshift medieval catapult. The rock shot through the glass door like a cannonball, missed Earl's head by two inches, and embedded itself clean into the kitchen drywall, leaving a perfect hole that would make a landlord weep.

The twenty feet of heavy-duty black duct tape, which had bravely trapped every bit of escaping atomic heat, started smoking like a cheap cigar. It unspooled itself in wild, flaming spirals, making the whole outside of the toaster wobble and twist like a junkyard dog's tail right before it gets a turkey leg.

Finally, the whole dang contraption shorted out spectacularly in a brilliant blue flame as thick smoke filled the house. Instead of a nice, evenly toasted Cherry Pop-Tart, the oven gave off a blinding flash that lit up the kitchen like the Fourth of July. It looked exactly like that time the teenage girl working the cheap highway fireworks stand had a baby and accidentally dropped her lit cigar into the mortar cannons.

As the smoke slowly cleared, Boon and Earl stood there completely covered in black soot, staring at the smoldering husk of the appliance. The only sound left was the faint, sad melting noise of the last strip of duct tape giving up on life and dripping onto the linoleum.

"Well," Boon concluded, calm as you please, reaching into the smoking ruin to yank the river rock out of the drywall. There was a completely charred, rock-hard Pop-Tart permanently glued to the side of it.

"Well, I'll be! That Pop-Tart we put in there is still cold as a well-digger's backside on the inside. Look here, Earl! We solved the uneven heat problem once and for all. It's now equally cold on both sides." He grinned through the soot as if he'd just invented sliced bread. "We might just as well drink up a few more beers. I'll have to go down to the Near-New thrift shop tomorrow and get another toaster oven."

Earl coughed up a cloud of black smoke. "Next time, we need a lighter stone. Maybe a river pebble wrapped in tinfoil, and definitely twice as much duct tape."

Boon nodded seriously, staring at the brand-new hole in his wall like it was a modern art exhibit. "Agreed. Now, where's that fishing line? We gotta fix the washing machine next. It's been makin' a funny noise again; sounds a lot like it's fixin' to flood the hog pen. Hey, you said your washing machine isn't working, too? We'd best get mine fixed and work on yours next. Need at least another twelve-pack of beer to get the engineering right."

He took a long pull from his warm beer, wiped his blackened mouth on his sleeve, and added with deep philosophical wisdom: "Earl, if it ain't broke, we just ain't tried hard enough yet."

Chapter Six:

Turkey Hunters: Sneakier Than a Coon, and more Jittery Than a Squirrel on Espresso

Boon took a long, loud slurp of his beer that sounded like a cypress swamp being drained through a rusty straw. He wiped his mouth with the exact same sleeve he'd used to clean the grease off the grill last month, then leaned back so far in his cheap plastic lawn chair that it let out a dangerous, plastic creak, threatening to launch him backward into the yard like a NASA rocket.

"Well now, Earl," he drawled, eyes narrowing, "let me tell ya somethin', and this here is the gospel truth, son. Straight from the Good Book of Poo-Dunk, Chapter One, Verse Two. Lord, have mercy on our souls. You wanna talk 'bout sneaky? The sneakiest critter walkin' on two legs ain't no coon, no sir. It's a dad-gum turkey hunter! I swear, they're worse than a wild fox that's been baptized in a henhouse full of Sunday school teachers.

You know darn good and well them fellers got about a million tall tales involving crawlin' under a rusty fence line on their belly like a copperhead snake with commitment issues, or straight-up commando-crawlin' through two miles of briars just to illegally pop a gobbler on somebody else's property. They'll chase a longbeard right into the middle of the state capitol building if they gotta, hollerin' 'Yeeeelp!' the whole way like it's their national battle cry. I swear, one of 'em would follow a wild turkey right into the aisle at Walmart and shoot the seasonal display." Boon paused to suck down half a glass of sweet tea.

"And don't even get me started on the sheer danger part of it. Them fellers ain't even human, Earl! They ain't got no self-control whatsoever. They oughta call 'em the most trigger-happy folks in the whole dad-burn huntin' business. They get so hopped up on the sound of a good 'yeeelp' or a cedar box call that they'll squeeze that trigger at anything that moves—even a passing cloud or a squirrel lookin' at 'em funny. They crawl around in the brush and will shoot directly into any bush that's actin' kind of shifty, thinkin' it might be hidin' a tom turkey with a twelve-inch beard.

Heck, look at ol' Cotton! Bless his heart. That poor fella has been peppered with birdshot more times than a kitchen colander's got holes, and every single time it was some jittery turkey hunter who mistook him for a big ol' tom struttin' through the hardwoods. I keep tellin' him not to make turkey sounds when he's walking through the woods!

Ain't nobody ever shoots Cotton during deer season! Not even once! Deer season has civilized, respectable hunters. You know how it is, Earl. You sit up in a nice wooden stand, sip hot black coffee, lie about the monster twelve-point buck that walked by at three hundred yards, and enjoy the social tradition of camp life with your buddies.

But a turkey hunter? Naw. He's a lone wolf. A solitary weirdo out there in the woods all by himself, wearin' so much camo he blends in with the moss, talkin' to bushes, arguin' with hoot owls, and makin' kissy noises at imaginary wild hens. I gotta give 'em this, Earl, they do seem to have fun in their own special, kinda stupid way. Because their huntin' stories sure don't start out like some low-country pity party.

You ain't never gonna hear a turkey hunter say, 'Well, I'd been sittin' in this ol' box stand for seven long hours, half-drunk on moonshine, gotta pee so bad my eyes are floatin', and then a doggone squirrel showed up and ruined everything.'

Nope! Their stories always start with a whole lot more hollerin', cussin', and the unmistakable sound of somebody fallin' butt-over-teakettle down a steep creek bank, followed immediately by Cotton screamin' bloody murder after gettin' shot in the backside again. They always say, 'I swear to God, officer, he looked and sounded just like a mature turkey!' Bless their little camo-covered hearts."

Boon paused, took another noisy swig from his glass, and grinned wide enough to show the dark gap where his front tooth used to be before the pliers incident.

"Tell you what, Earl. If those turkey hunters ever get organized, the rest of us had better hide in the storm cellar. Till then, pass me another beer. I reckon we oughta go deer huntin' next weekend."

Earl nodded, chuckling deeply into his own aluminum can. "Amen to that, brother. Amen to that." He gave a deep, satisfied nod as they clinked their cans together, watching the hot southern sun dip low behind the loblolly pines.

CHAPTER SEVEN:

DIT AND WILLY

Boon has some neighbors, and the Lord knows they keep life interesting 'round these parts.

Right across the gravel road lives the one and only Dit, short for "Dit I tell ya? I knows that already!"

It doesn't matter what the topic of conversation is—weather rolling in from the county line, diesel prices crawling up like a possum on a fence post, or the mysterious situation where a neighbor's prize cow somehow escaped, wandered across two barbed-wire pastures, and personally selected your truck bed as its private restroom of choice. As soon as you open your mouth to start talking, Dit leans way back in her porch chair like she's already completely bored with the information. One eye squints shut tight like she's sighting down a rusted shotgun barrel at your sentence before it's even finished.

Then comes that slow, highly practiced spit—a perfect little stream of Skoal dark juice launched with the deadly, mechanical accuracy of a professional lawn sprinkler set on high. She waves you off halfway through your story like she's swatting a pesky horsefly.

Then comes the inevitable: "Dit I tell ya? I knows it already!"

And you'll be standing there in the dirt thinking, No ma'am, you absolutely did not, because I just watched that black-and-white cow commit the crime thirty minutes ago with my own two eyes.

But she ain't done. Not by a long shot. She'll nod slowly, like a hanging judge who's already read the verdict, sentenced you to the gallows, and eaten a full ham lunch before the trial even started.

"Yup," she says, smug as all get-out. "I saw it comin'."

"Seen what comin'?" Boon asks, completely against his better judgment.

"The storm. The diesel prices. That cow's exact gastrointestinal problem. All of it."

Apparently, it was all written in the wind, the clouds, and the specific way the gas station hot-dog rollers squeak on a Tuesday morning. Dit can read local omens like other folks read the sports page. If anyone tries to explain the details further—say, mention that the same runaway cow also stepped directly on your cooler and ate half your live fish bait—she'll just squint the other eye this time, like she's adjusting the crosshairs on a scope for a longer shot, and hit you with, "Mumm. Just like I said. Dit I say I knowed it?"

Boon usually looks around blankly at that point—at a fence post, maybe at the dog—just to make sure reality and sanity still exist. But by then, Dit's already leaning back again, smug as a porch cat in a sunbeam, acting like she personally scheduled the entire sequence of cosmic events just to prove she was right all along.

The whole county calls her Dit now. Even her own mama finally gave up and just writes "Dit" on her birthday cards. If that gal won the state lottery tomorrow, the local newspaper headline would read: "Local Woman Dit I-Knowed-I-Would-Win-Already Hits Jackpot. Says she won't quit her job because nobody else in the county knows how to set up the fried chicken lunch buffet at the truck stop right."

Her name started all the way back in third grade when old Mrs. Hoe asked the class what sound a frog makes. Little Brenda Kay shot her hand up in the air and hollered, "Dit I know it already! Ribbit!" before anybody else got a single chance to breathe.

The next question was two plus two. Brenda Kay's hand went right back up. Mrs. Hoe sighed heavily and said, "Yes, Brenda?"

"Dit, I knew it. The answer is four."

When Mrs. Hoe asked, "What star will guide you north?" Brenda's hand waved like a flag in a hurricane. Before the poor teacher could even open her mouth, half the classroom muttered in perfect unison, "Dit knows it already."

The teacher tried to shush them, but it was far too late. The name Dit stuck harder than chewing gum on a velvet church pew in the middle of December. By high school, she was answering to it like it was printed on her legal birth certificate. At the Friday night football games, the PA announcer would boom over the speaker: "And that spectacular tackle was brought to you by Dit-I-Know-It-Already Daddy's Used-Car Lot! Where the deals are fair and the coffee's free. You can even trade in a working mule!"

Then came the Internet age. Somebody—probably her second cousin Ray Junior—convinced her that you could get email through regular paper mail. All she had to do was buy a brand-new computer, and the physical letters would start rolling into her mailbox. Since Dit loves mail-order catalogs and clearinghouse sweepstakes, she marched right down to the Walmart in the next county, bought herself one of those big silver desktop towers with the rainbow Windows sticker, and lugged it home in the trunk of her mama's dented Buick like it was a sack of sweet chicken feed. She set it up right on the kitchen table, plugged it in, and waited.

The very next morning, she's standing out by the road in her faded housecoat and fuzzy pink slippers, her morning coffee going cold in her hand. Old Mr. Purvis—known affectionately across the county as Perv—rolls up on his mail route, sixty-nine years old and still surviving the heat.

Dit hollers, "Where's my email at, Perv?"

Purvis blinks through his thick bifocals. "Your what?"

"My email! I've been waitin' two weeks! I got me a computer and everything!"

He tries to explain, Lord bless him. "Honey, the only thing I know about those computer contraptions is they got mice. Get yourself some d-CON poison or a wooden trap."

Dit narrows her eyes like he just told her the moon is made of processed Velveeta cheese. "You holdin' out on me, Perv? I know you got a canvas bag back there with my physical email in it!"

This went on for fifteen straight days. She'd stand by the ditch and cuss him six ways to Sunday, yelling things like, "You sorry, lazy sack of government waste!" Mr. Purvis would just quietly hand over her electric bill and a tractor catalog while he prayed to God for early retirement.

Finally, on day fifteen, she comes stomping out to the road in the same stained housecoat, her hair looking like a midnight raccoon convention, waving a piece of paper she'd managed to print from Hotmail like it was the ancient Dead Sea Scrolls.

"I knew it!" she yells at the top of her lungs. "Y'all been holdin' my email hostage in the back of that mail truck! Look right here! It says: Welcome to Hotmail, Dit I-know-already! It's got my whole official name and everything! Where is my email? She screams. Perv hits the gas and runs away like a frightened cow with a swarm of hornets on its butt."

Then she finally hired the teenage boy up the hill to show her how to actually operate the machine. Now she's got Wi-Fi and everything—calls it "the Wi-Fis"—and sends mass chain emails about Jesus, essential oils, and miracle alligator-grease face creams to half the county. The subject line always reads: "FWD: FWD: FWD: Dit I-know-already sent you this because she loves you." And every last one of us in Poo-Dunk replies with "Say what?" just to watch the glorious digital chaos unfold.

Down the road near the rusty railroad tracks, just past the yellow traffic light that's been blinking since the President Ike administration, lives a fine shade-tree mechanic named Flat Tire Willy. He operates out of a leaning tin garage that looks like it lost a heavy fistfight with a Category 5 tornado. The crooked, hand-painted wooden sign out front reads:

WILLY'S FIX-IT. IF I CAN'T FIX IT, IT AIN'T BROKE (OR IT'S A LIVE HORSE).

Anyone with a blown flat tire, a sputtering carburetor, or a mysterious metal clunk that sounds like a skeleton doing the Macarena inside the wheel well eventually ends up at Willy's. He's got the only tire-changing machine in all of Poo-Dunk County. It's a 1948 iron beast that groans, pops, and wheezes like your heavy uncle after Thanksgiving dinner, but it still spins truer than most politicians on election day.

You roll up into the gravel yard, and there's Willy, half-buried under somebody's rusted hood, a cigarette dangling precariously from his bottom lip, black grease up to his elbows. He looks like he was born wearing a stained Dale Earnhardt T-shirt and has never taken it off for a wash. He pokes his head out from the engine bay, squints through thick eyebrows that have their own distinct zip code, and growls in a low voice that sounds like rough gravel soaked in used motor oil:

"Want me to fix it, or are you just here to jaw some?"

You hand over your keys and take a cautious step back, like you just dropped off a wild raccoon that might still be alive, highly offended, and ready to fight for its life.

"Here for an oil change," you say nervously.

Willy wipes his hands on a rag that used to be a cotton T-shirt sometime during the early Clinton administration. He squints deep under the hood like he's negotiating a complex peace treaty with the firing cylinders.

"Yup," he says after a long, agonizing pause. "Be about an hour or so."

You glance around the dark shop while you wait in the heat. That's when you notice the massive, rusted 55-gallon oil drum sitting in the corner with a crooked label written in thick black Sharpie that reads: "USED OIL – DO NOT DRINK." Next to it is another dented barrel labeled "MAYBE GASOLINE – SMELLS FUNNY, PROBABLY FINE," and a third mysterious one simply marked "MYSTERY FLUID – GOOD FOR EVERYTHING EXCEPT MARRIAGE."

The tin walls are decorated with faded, peeling NASCAR posters, a wooden sign that reads Camp Quityourbitchin, and a grease-stained paper calendar from 1957 that still proudly displays Miss October in all her retro glory. Willy likes the vintage picture because she happens to be wearing a very nice, traditional straw hat—which also happens to be the only piece of clothing she is wearing on the entire page.

Tools are scattered absolutely everywhere across the dirt floor; a few hang neatly on pegboards, but most are just sitting wherever they happened to land when Willy threw them. If you're brave enough to wander into the dark back corner of Boon's "shop"—which is really just a collapsing barn with severe delusions of grandeur—you'll find the absolute crown jewel of the whole mechanical operation: an old plaid couch that looks like it lost a brutal highway fight with a semi-truck full of heavy motor oil.

This glorious, sagging beast of a couch, Willy firmly insists, is placed there exclusively for "customer comfort." He says it with a completely straight face, like he's running a luxury Mercedes dealership in Atlanta instead of a greasy junkyard chop shop.

Everyone in Poo-Dunk knows the real truth: that couch is Willy's official Post-Lunch Recovery Center. After a long, hardworking morning that usually wraps up around 10:45 a.m., Willy treats himself to his signature gourmet mechanic's lunch: four cold, cheap beers and a stack of bologna sandwiches thick enough to choke a wild goat. Then he waddles over to the corner, kicks his work boots off—releasing a pungent foot smell that could strip the clear-coat right off a fender—and crashes onto the couch cushions like a felled redwood tree.

There is enough ancient grease and oil soaked into that couch to lubricate nine rusty farm trucks at the exact same time. The cushions have achieved a permanent, wet-look synthetic shine over the decades. If you make the mistake of sitting on it, you'll stand back up three pounds heavier and permanently stained for life. Scientists could study the strata of organic crud on those cushions like ancient sedimentary rock—there are documented layers from the Roosevelt administration embedded deep in the springs.

Earl Ray once made the fatal mistake of sitting on it during high school football season. He stood up two hours later with a perfect, greasy imprint of his butt on the fabric and a mysterious new dark, tattoo-like grease mark on his jeans that still won't wash out to this day.

Willy just grinned through his beard, let out a massive burp, and said, "See there? Customer comfort. You look relaxed as hell, buddy."

The man's mechanical and sanitary standards are lower than a copperhead snake's belly in a ditch, but somehow, between his afternoon naps and his bologna comas, he keeps the whole chaotic operation running. Barely. God bless the beautiful, greasy disasters of the world.

While you're standing there trying not to inhale too deeply because the shop smells like a unique perfume of burnt oil, stale cigarette smoke, and deep life regrets, Willy suddenly lets out a victorious whoop from underneath the hood.

"Found your problem!" he hollers, banging a wrench against the radiator. "You got a loose… uh… thingama-indicator. Classic case."

He emerges from the engine bay holding a small, incredibly greasy metal part that looks suspiciously like it was hacked off an old John Deere riding lawnmower.

"Thirty bucks for the part, twenty for the labor, and fifty bucks for me not telling your wife about the pair of pink panties I found under your driver's seat."

You immediately try to bargain. "Come on now, Willy, that's outright highway robbery."

He grins wide, showing off a solid gold tooth that probably started its life as a Champion spark plug. "Highway robbery? Boy, this is Poo-Dunk County. Round here, we call it 'fair market value plus a little extra for my professional expert opinion.'"

While he's tightening things up, Willy likes to entertain his waiting clients with educational lectures. Today's topic is the fundamental differences between "city mechanics" and "real mechanics."

"them city boys got them fancy computerized machines that plug into your truck and tell 'em what's wrong via a screen. Me? I listen to the soul of the engine. If it sounds like a dying alley cat spinning around in a clothes dryer, it's the timing belt. If it sounds like my third ex-wife grinding her teeth and screaming about alimony, it's the transmission. Simple as that."

He spits a stream of dark tobacco juice into an old Maxwell House coffee can with terrifying, Olympic-level accuracy, then continues working. Next to it sits another identical coffee can full of random rusty bolts, washers, and at least one plastic thing that looks suspiciously like it came off a backyard lawn chair.

You point your finger at the spare parts can. "What's that specific bolt from?"

Willy shrugs his shoulders care-free. "Dunno. But it was definitely holdin' somethin' together before it fell out. It's comfortin' to never know when a bolt gets lost or just becomes an extra, you know?"

You stare at him blankly, thinking to yourself: Comfortin? Extra? On a brake line?

Meanwhile, he's topping off your vital fluids like a mad scientist wielding a crescent wrench. He pours in a little splash of 10W-30, a dash of chainsaw bar oil, and maybe a literal spoonful of leftover bacon grease he saved from his breakfast biscuit wrapper.

"Lubrication's lubrication, boy," he says, real confident-like, wiping his dipstick on his shirt.

He talks constantly as he works. "Last week, some rich fella from Atlanta brought in a brand-new, fancy foreign SUV. The computer diagnostics in the city told him it needed a

$1,200 electronic sensor. I told him to hold his horses, crawled underneath the chassis with a beer, and tightened one single regular bolt that had vibrated loose on the dirt roads. Charged him fifty bucks and a six-pack of premium beer. He left here thinkin' I was a certified genius. Truth is, I just know which bolts them city boys always forget to tighten."

An hour later—or three, depending entirely on how many tall stories he feels like telling and how many cold beers he's cracked open—Willy slams the heavy steel hood down with absolute authority.

"She's good as new," he declares proudly. "Might leak a little oil on your driveway for the first week, but that's just her way of saying she appreciates the personal attention. If it starts making a new noise on the highway, just bring her back. If it's a light rattling sound, ignore it. If it's a heavy grinding sound, ignore it harder. If the whole engine explodes... well, that one's on you, buddy. Go buy another truck."

"Just remember, duct tape and an honest prayer will fix about 90% of things in this life. If that doesn't work, bring it back here, and I'll hit it with a much bigger hammer."

Right as he says that, a small, unidentified metal piece falls out from underneath your bumper and clatters onto the gravel. You stare down at it, then look back at him. "Was that important?"

Willy studies the piece for a single second, spits his tobacco, and tosses it casually into a scrap metal can. "Don't know if it was. We'll find out pretty quick on your drive home. Come again!"

You drive away slowly, knowing for a fact that the flatbed tow truck following a mile behind you belongs to Willy's brother.

Now, a week later, word of his mechanical genius got around faster than bad gossip at the town beauty parlor. Folks are now driving from three counties over just to get some of Willy's famous "moonshine and air service." You can pull into the yard with a dangerously hissing tire, and leave thirty minutes later with exactly 38 psi in the rubber, a mason jar of clear liquid that smells like paint thinner, and a firm handshake.

Local rumor has it that one guy showed up in a brand-new luxury BMW and asked Willy for high-end synthetic oil. Willy just stared at the car owner like the man had requested fresh unicorn tears.

Then Willy stepped up, whispered some sweet nothings directly to the aluminum engine block like it was an old high school flame, tightened a random bolt, and left a massive, greasy handprint right on the pristine clean fenders. For good measure, he slammed his hand on the horn to test it, then nodded approvingly before handing over the keys with a cryptic, gold-toothed grin:

"She'll purr like a prize kitten now, hoss. That'll be thirty bucks."

The German car sputtered, let out a loud pop from the exhaust, and then sped off down the highway like a fighter jet.

Friends, this is exactly why Flat Tire Willy is a certified local legend in Poo-Dunk. He may not own a fancy computer diagnostic tool or a clean shirt, but he's got a heavy hammer, a wild attitude, and a cooler full of ice-cold "roadside sodas." In Poo-Dunk County, that is better than a factory warranty on any given day of the week.

Chapter Eight:

Porch Talk is Important

Lord have mercy, Boon's porch looks like a hillbilly nightmare that got drunk, fell down the mountain, and decided to set up permanent camp. It's less of a porch and more of an ecosystem where discarded junk goes to evolve into new, terrifying life forms.

You've got at least five broken recliners lined up like stadium seating, each one missing vital parts, arms, backs, or cushions. One of them is held together with so much baling wire it could probably pick up radio stations from 1973. There's a coffee table made out of a truck tailgate sitting on cinder blocks, permanently sticky from years of spilled sweet tea, snacks, beer, and chewing tobacco juice.

The floorboards are decorated with a fine mosaic of crushed beer cans, bottle caps, and the occasional chicken feather. Empty feed sacks flap in the breeze like sad little flags of surrender. A rusted-out chest freezer hums in the corner; it isn't plugged in, mind you—it's just where Boon stores his "extra" fishing bait and the emergency case of beer "for company" (which somehow never lasts past Wednesday).

Willy's contribution to this architectural disaster is a tower of motor oil cans stacked like a modern sculpture next to a pile of old tires that the goats have claimed as their personal jungle gym. One ambitious goat is usually perched on top like a furry gargoyle, staring at visitors with pure criminal intent.

Earl Ray likes to "help" by leaving his collection of half-finished projects scattered everywhere: a lawnmower engine in a baby pool, three fishing rods missing reels, and a mysterious, leaking bucket labeled "Do Not Open" that occasionally makes a faint whistling sound.

The whole porch sags in the middle like it's exhausted from carrying the weight of their life choices. And every evening, Boon, Earl Ray, Stinker John, Willy, and you settle into your respective recliners like it's the most luxurious resort in the county—swatting mutant flies, passing around a bag of stale pork rinds, and arguing over whether the turkey in the pen is plotting an escape or telepathically controlling the garage door opener.

Boon always says, "This here's my outdoor livin' room. Got better ventilation than the house, and the view doesn't judge me none."

As we sat there, the porch was loaded with fellers listening to Stinker John, who was spitting teeth-rattling truths.

“Y'all wanna hear 'bout the dang craziest thing to ever stumble through Poo-Dunk?” Stinker John started, waving a half-eaten pickled egg. “Lemme tell you, this ain't no story for the faint o' heart, and it sho' nuff ain't a story 'bout GOOD decision-making. Well, now, picture this: it was early last Saturday mornin’, still darker than the inside of a coal mine, or the inside of Earl’s barbecue smoker after he tried that 'extra hickory experiment' that nearly smoked the county fair judges clean unconscious. Gather 'round the cracker barrel for this one.

It happened at our local Poo-Dunk liquor store—you know the one, right between the bait shop and the place that sells used tractor tires that look like dinosaur sheds. The place was supposed to be shut up tighter than a drum on a Sunday morning. Double-locked, alarm set, steel shutters down. A sign on the door big as a barn said CLOSED, and it even had one of those little paper clock signs saying, 'Back at 9 a.m.' with a note reading, 'Don't even think about it.'

But lo and behold, here comes this feller. Dressed like a masked bandit, bless his heart. Must've been blind as a bat or drunker than Cooter Brown before he even started. Maybe he figured the sign was just a suggestion, or maybe his thirst hit him like a freight train. Either way, subtlety was not in this boy's vocabulary.

He busted through that back door with the grace of a bull in a china shop that'd already had three Red Bulls and a divorce. Glass was shattering, and the alarm was whooping like a cat with its tail stepped on, but did that slow him down? Heck no. This rascal had a mission.

He wasn't there for no fancy French wine with a cork and a name nobody can pronounce. No sir. His eyes went straight to the bottom shelf—the sacred land of the real good stuff. Right there, next to the fifty-cent wine that tastes like battery acid, sat Old Blaster Whiskey. That legendary brown bottle contains pure fire. On most bottles, the label is half-peeled off, and a single drink will make you see double, question your life choices, and occasionally speak fluent French to farm equipment.

Well, that bandit didn't waste time with formalities like a glass or even a plastic cup. He was grabbin' them pint bottles as if they owed him money. Glug-glug-glug! He wasn't just tippin' 'em back, neither; he was slammin' 'em down like he was playing championship dominoes with pint bottles. BAM, BAM, BAM! Each empty one clattered to the floor like a drunk orchestra.

By the time the sheriff rolled up—lights flashin', siren blarin', and still half-asleep—our boy was sittin' in the middle of the aisle, mask halfway down his face, surrounded by a mountain of empty Old Blaster bottles, trying to teach a stray raccoon how to sing the high notes in 'Sweet Home Alabama'.

When they asked him why he did it, he just grinned that sloppy, whiskey-soaked grin, burped a blue flame, and said, “Well hell, officer... the sign said closed, but my liver said open 24 hours.”

They hauled him off, still clutching one bottle like it was his firstborn. Last I heard, the judge gave him community service at the liquor store. Now he stocks the bottom shelf, which is basically like putting a fox in charge of security at the local egg factory.”

Chapter Nine:

Cheers

Friday night in Poo-Dunk means one thing: high school football under those old stadium lights that buzz louder than a hive of angry hornets on Red Bull. The mosquitoes are out in full force, big enough to file flight plans, carry off small children, and demand their own parking spaces. The air is thick with the sacred aroma of popcorn, boiled peanuts, and deep-fried regrets.

The aluminum bleachers are packed tighter than a church pew during a free-will offering. Every squeak sounds exactly like ninety-nine-year-old Uncle Dale's knees trying to stand up after Sunday dinner. Half the town is here to watch the game. The other half is here to see who's dating whom and to check if their ex-spouse showed up with someone they met at the bait shop.

Down on the track, the cheer squad is giving it everything they've got—and when I say "everything," I mean gravity, momentum, and several local seismic monitoring stations know they are cheering.

There are four of them: four proud, two-hundred-and-fifty-pound cheerleaders in matching neon-orange uniforms working harder than the offensive line. They're jumping and clapping with the determined look of shopping carts with one bad wheel that refuses to be stopped by basic laws of physics.

Here is the cheer:

"WE AIN'T FANCY! WE AIN'T RICH! BUT OUR TEAM CAN DIG A DITCH!"

Clap-clap. STOMP.

Clap-clap. STOMP. Clap-clap. STOMP.

The stomps hit so hard that the concession stand attendant has to steady the nacho cheese warmer to keep it from vibrating off the counter.

The cheer continues:

"THEY'RE WEARIN' HELMETS! SHINY AND GOLD! THEY IS THE BEST DANG STORY EVER TOLD!"

One of the girls attempts a high kick, gets halfway up, thinks better of it, and smoothly converts the move into what cheerleading experts would call a "controlled, enthusiastic wobble" that temporarily alters the local gravitational pull. The crowd doesn't care one bit. Most of these people are relatives anyway, and the boys in the stands are only here hoping to get a date or a free funnel cake after the game.

From the concession stand, some proud daddy yells, "Get 'em, Tammy!" which is confusing because three of the four cheerleaders are named Tammy.

The squad launches into the next cheer, arms swinging like windmills in a Category 5 hurricane:

"HEAR THAT SOUND? IT'S THE POO-DUNK BEAT! GONNA KNOCK THAT BALL RIGHT OFF ITS FEET!"

The marching band keeps the beat, but the tuba player just dropped his funnel cake inside his instrument, creating a tragic, greasy muffled thud. Somewhere in the brass section, a trumpet squeaks like it's personally offended by the lack of musical talent around it.

Meanwhile, one brave Tammy attempts a small jump. It registers on the Richter scale as a solid 4.2. The PA announcer actually pauses for a second like he's waiting for the aftershocks to pass.

"Y'all lookin' thirsty?" the PA announcer booms, his voice crackling with static. "We got red hots and cold beer at the sideline! Y'all lookin' slow? Shining helmets! GO! GO! GO!"

The cheerleaders wrap it up with a big clap that is technically synchronized if you close your eyes and count to three very slowly. The final stomp sends a visible ripple through the bleachers, causing Old Man Jenkins to spill his hot sauce right into his lap.

The crowd erupts as if they just witnessed Olympic gymnastics instead of four determined girls fighting a losing battle with Newton's laws.

Old Man Jenkins leans over to his buddy and says loudly, "Boy, that's school spirit right there! How 'bout them good-lookin' gals!" His wife hands him his glasses without saying a word, shaking her head.

Right about then, the Poo-Dunk Fighting Possums ran onto the field. The team bursts through the giant paper banner—that is, except for three linemen who immediately trip over the remains of it and form a human pile-up at the 20-yard line. The mascot, a very sweaty feller in a moth-eaten possum costume that smells like damp basement, gets accidentally body-slammed by the entire offensive line.

The cheerleaders don't miss a single beat, switching seamlessly into: "DIG! THAT! DITCH! Go, go, go, you Possums!"

Halftime hits like a freight train full of sweet tea and hot sauce. The scoreboard mercifully clicks over to 28–0 in favor of the visitors, and the PA announcer, who sounds like he'd been chain-smoking since third grade, booms, "Folks, it's halftime! Stick around for the Poo-Dunk High Marching Band and the Fighting Possum Cheerleaders!"

The three Tammys, plus the one non-Tammy named Limmy, waddle to the center of the field like they were about to perform an exorcism on the 50-yard line.

First up: the marching band. They launch into their signature arrangement of "Dixie" with a surprise key change that nobody saw coming, least of all the clarinet section, who are now playing what sounds like a cat being squeezed. The tuba player, still recovering from the funnel cake incident, hits a low note so deep it makes three dogs in the parking lot start howling in perfect harmony and unlocks two car alarms.

Then the cheerleaders take center stage for the main event. They drag out a giant handmade banner that reads "GO POSSUMS! WE AIN'T DEAD YET!" in glitter and what appears to be leftover lime-green barn paint. Two of the girls hold it up while the other two attempt what they call "the pyramid."

It starts promisingly. Tammy #1 climbs onto the shoulders of Tammy #2 and Tammy #3, who lock arms and plant their feet like they were trying to hold back a Category 3 hurricane. Then Limmy—the smallest cheerleader at only 230 pounds—climbs up there, arms spread wide like she was about to deliver the Sermon on the Mount.

"WE ARE THE POSSUMS! HEAR US ROAR!" she yells.

The tuba players give a collective blast that can be heard in three counties. For one glorious second, the pyramid actually holds. The crowd goes completely wild.

Then gravity remembers its job.

The whole structure lists hard to starboard. Limmy on top lets out a heroic "WHOA NELLY!" and tries to correct by windmilling her arms like she's directing airport traffic during a blizzard. The base staggers three steps sideways, looking like a mule that drank a gallon of bad rum.

The pyramid didn't so much collapse as it surrendered with dignity. All four girls go down in a glorious, slow-motion pile of sequins, mud, and sweat—looking like four sacks of sweet potatoes hitting a trampoline.

The crowd loses their minds, cheering, whistling, and hollering like it was the best thing they'd seen since the '88 state championship (which they also lost due to a rogue tractor on the field). Undeterred, the cheerleaders pop right back up, brushing grass and unidentified stadium debris off their uniforms, grinning like heroes.

"THAT'S ALL RIGHT! THAT'S OKAY! YOU'LL BE DIGGIN' DITCHES ANYWAY!" they chant aggressively at the visiting team's sideline.

Next comes the special halftime stunt: "The Possum Roll." One of the Tammys is supposed to do a graceful cartwheel while the others hold up a giant stuffed possum. Instead, the attempted front handspring is wildly misjudged, turning into an accidental barrel roll that carries her halfway to the 30-yard line like a runaway bowling ball. She pops up holding the stuffed possum like a war trophy and yells, "TOUCHDOWN, BABY!"

To close out the show, they bring out the school's pride and joy: an ancient Civil War cannon that has barely ever worked and is mostly used for storing stray gravel. The cheerleaders gather around it, shaking pom-poms and chanting, "BOOM! BOOM! POSSUM DOOM!"

The cannon actually fires this time… sort of. It makes a sad, wet humpppp sound and shoots out a massive cloud of black smoke along with what looks suspiciously like old confetti mixed with dryer lint and a stray sock. A single plastic possum flies out about six feet, lands with a thud, and melts instantly on the turf.

The crowd gives them a standing ovation anyway.

As the girls jog off the field, still breathing hard and waving as if they'd just won Olympic gold, Boon turns to Earl, shaking his head with pure, unadulterated admiration.

"Earl, I swear them girls got more heart than the whole offensive line. They fell, got up, and still managed to insult the other team on the way out. That's Poo-Dunk spirit right there."

Earl takes a long sip of his lukewarm beer and nods. "Yep. Physics is undefeated tonight."

Down on the field, one of the Tammys is already yelling at the team as they trudge back out for the second half: "DIG! THAT! DITCH! YOU SON OF A POSSUM! GO, TEAM, GO!"

The scoreboard stays at 28–0 because the scorekeeper ran off with his second cousin at the end of the second quarter, so no one truly knows who won. The game ends as it always does in Poo-Dunk: the kissing cousins go home together, the lights flicker out, and the local police come to break up the fights in the gravel parking lot.

Chapter Ten:

Moonshine Mudcats

Local Radio Comedy Broadcast

STYLE: Lo-fi, folksy AM-station chaos, narrated by Cletus

RUN TIME: Approx. 6–7 minutes

The loudspeaker booms:

"Ladies and gentlemen, boys and girls, grab yer popcorn, hold onto yer hats, and hide yer coolers! 'Cause it's time for your hometown heroes, the Moonshine Mudcats, to take the field!"

Pitcher — Buster Mazy!

"Ol' Wild Buster's climbin' up to the mound, wobblin' like a three-legged coon dog on an icy porch! Now, if he can stay upright long enough to throw one, you're in for a show. That knuckleball ain't just wicked — it's spiritual. I've seen preachers cry and batters quit the game after facin' that thing!"

Behind the Plate — Ol' Fat Bob!

"He's squatting behind home like a Brahma bull protecting his salt lick. Ain't nothin' gettin' past that wall of man. A runner comes to slide home, they're bouncing off him like roadkill on a semi's grill! That's right, folks. Fat Bob anchors this team like a trailer hitch at a monster truck rally!"

Over at First Base — Boon!

"Stretchin' like he's made of taffy and forgettin' the count for the hundredth time tonight! He's hollering' at the ump again, something' about goggles while tossin' the ball like a one-armed hillbilly slinging' a corncob in a windstorm! And yep, straight into the beer cooler again. Classic Boon!"

Second Base — Skinny Jimbo Bob!

"Now folks, if you look closely—well, if you can look closely—you'll see Ol' Skinny Jimbo spazzin' around like a bullfrog wired to a car battery! There he goes, dancing' the hokey-pokey out there, arms and knees goin' every direction! And here comes his highlight... Fwahh! That man's spitting' loogies big enough to hydroplane on. Runners try slidin' into second and end up skating' through his personal spit swamp like a drunk raccoon on black ice!"

Third Base — Stinker John!

"Lordy, hold your noses, folks. Stinker's on duty! That boy doesn't care where the ball's hit, he's haulin' tail straight to third no matter what! You could hit it onto the moon, and he'd still dive headfirst into that bag! And the smell? Whew! The air gets thick enough to butter. Even the ump's gaggin' behind his mask! If you see a runner stop short halfway to third, you'll know why!"

Shortstop — Backdoor Hoyt!

"There he is, sneaky as a raccoon at a church picnic! Fastest hands this side of the county line—ball disappears faster'n Aunt Eloweez's peach schnapps. He's got those thick glasses makin' his eyes look like fried eggs under a magnifier, but don't let that fool ya. He tags runners out before they even think about sliding'. Says he can see 'em coming' from the corner of his eye, crediting it all to eatin' squirrel brains as a kid. Don't question genius, folks."

Left Field — Squealin' Squirrel Jonny!

"Ah, look at him! Pickin' flowers again. Bless his heart, that boy's more distracted than a dog with a laser pointer. But when that ball finally heads his way... SWEET MERCY! He lets out a squeal that'll make a hog faint! You'll hear the play before you see it, guaranteed!"

Center Field — One-Eye Jack!

"King of the outfield right there. That patch of dirt's his kingdom, mostly 'because nobody else wants to go near it. With just one good peeper, Jack chases pop flies like they're UFOs. Never lands where he expects, but when he catches one, you'd think he just won the dang lottery! Word to the wise: if Jack's throwin', duck first, celebrate later."

In Right Field — The Legend Himself, Toothless Sammy!

"The crowd favorite, bringin' his patented 'Wind-Up and Wind-Down!' That's right, every pitch comes with its own soundtrack: one part growl, two parts gas-powered symphony. When he gets riled up, he'll throw a laser beam that could char the grass, and if you're sittin' downwind, well, God bless ya and hold your nose."

"There they are, ladies and gentlemen, your Moonshine Mudcats! A little rough, a little rowdy, and a whole lotta unforgettable. So, crack open a cold one and hang on... 'cause this here ballgame's fixin' to get ugly in all the right ways!"

THE MOONSHINE MUDCATS VS. THE POO-DUNK SHINING HELMETS

[00:00] – INTRO MUSIC

(A twangy country guitar riff. Static pops. Rooster crow + crowd hum.)

CLETUS (over music, enthusiastic drawl):

"Well, howdy there, sports fans and random folks who still ain't found their remote! This here's Cletus 'Catfish' Hollerbee, comin' at you live from sunny—well, mostly dusty—Poo-Dunk County Field! Sponsored by Uncle Boo-Boo's Bait & Bankruptcy loans!

Not to mention—I already know it, 'cause it's my Daddy's car lot—remember, folks, you always get a fair deal. Buy a truck and get a coupon for twenty-five dollars that's good at Tire Willy's repair shop.

Tonight's matchup: your Moonshine Mudcats versus the pride of three townships and a gas station—the Poo-Dunk Shining Helmets! Now let's get this circus rollin'!"

[00:25] – INNING THREE: "The Action Heats Up"

(SFX: Crowd chatter, beer cans popping, bat tapping)

CLETUS:

"Up next—Stinker John! The crowd loves him almost as much as they hate sitting' downwind. Last week, this fella tried to steal third base when the bases were emptier than Cousin Dale's savings jar, but let's see what he's got tonight!"

(SFX: Pitcher winds, slow whoosh, bat CRACKS)

CLETUS:

"He connects! That ball's floatin' high… higher… Lord, it's hanging' like Mama's laundry in a storm! Left fielder's lookin' up, lookin' down, now diggin' through his pockets for sunglasses! Crap! HE DROPPED IT!

Boon's tearing' for second, but now he's stopped' mid-run to ARGUE with the second baseman about light beer versus brown liquor! Folks, you can't make this stuff up.

Stinker John slides safely to first, puffing like a prize hog. That's an official Poo-Dunk Error! And unofficially, the funniest thing I've seen since Aunt Patty tried to referee a pie-eatin' contest."

[01:45] – A WILD INTERRUPTION

CLETUS:

"Now stridin' up—it's One-Eye Jack! He's got one good eye and half-good judgment. The pitcher winds, here comes the throw. He SWINGS! And wait—he hit his own knee! Jack's hoppin' like a frog on jumper cables!

Hold up now! He's spotted a coon runnin' across the infield! He's got the bat, chasin' it full-speed! We got our first Coon Delay of the season! Fat Bob's runnin' outta the dugout with a fishin' net! Lordy, this field looks like Saturday night at the county fair!"

(SFX: Crowd roaring, possum screech, net whoosh, metallic clank)

CLETUS:

"The umpire calls time—he's eatin' a corn dog and questionin' his life choices. Folks, if chaos were a sport, this team'd be undefeated!"

[02:40] – THE BIG FINISH (KINDA)

CLETUS:

"Finally, it's our fan-favorite Toothless Sammy—grinnin', gummin', and geared up! Bases look like a family picnic that's gone wrong. The wind-up… the pitch… CRACK! Foul ball straight up! CLONK! Oh, sweet biscuits, it's nailed Squealin' Jonny in the bullpen! He's snortin' like a hog again, bless him.

Sammy gets another swing… the pitcher tosses… POINK! Little bloop drop between short and center! Boon scores! Stinker scores! And here comes One-Eye Jack, a beer still under his hat... HE SCORES TOO!

Sammy's roundin' second, forgot his helmet, crowd's goin' wild! They're callin' it a Triple-Decker Poo-Dunk Home Run! Scoreboard says 3-0, but truth is, we're all just losin' track and lovin' it!"

[03:55] – BOTTOM OF THE FIFTH: "The Sun's Gone and So's the Logic"

CLETUS (clearing throat):

"Well, the ump just declared this the final inning 'cause the sun's gone down faster than a hound dog after a squirrel, and the place has run clean outta beer. Fat Bob says he's the only one keepin' score. He's tallyin' cans, not runs—says it reflects his average. That's dedication, if not hydration!"

(SFX: Belch, crowd laughter)

[04:25] – THE FINAL OUTS

CLETUS:

"New pitcher: Wild Bill. He's lookin' loose—maybe too loose, kinda twitchy. He throws the ball... THUD! It lands right on the porta-potty! Folks, that's a Poo-Dunk Outhouse Special!

Next pitch! Batter swings at a dragonfly! He's missin' it by a yard, maybe seein' double or seein' his ex-wife (same effect). Walk issued! Batter jogs halfway before Wild Bill remembers to argue with himself about trajectory—claims he meant to throw backward! I swear, this man's a philosophical pitcher."

(SFX: Arguing in background, bottle shatters, crowd: "YEE-HAW!")

CLETUS:

"New batter's Brandy Randy. Look at that mullet glistening in the stadium lights. Wild Bill squints, sets, and fires his fastball... WHAM! Line drive toward short! Backdoor Hoyt dives—look at that form! Rolls, pops up, he's got it! Now throws... OH, SWEET MARY! Ball's over the backstop, right into Mrs. Gable's petunia patch!"

(SFX: Garden tools clatter)

MRS. GABLE (shouting off-mic):

"MY PETUNIAS, YOU IDIOT! You made me soil my panties, too!"

CLETUS (laughing fit):

"And there you have it! Hoyt's aim is as crooked as a politician's handshake!"

[05:45] – THE FINALE

(SFX: Crowd cheering, harmonica flourish)

CLETUS:

"The ump signals 'safe' toward the beer cooler—that's official play stoppage! Final score's somewhere around 4 to 2, depending on who's countin' and how much they've had to drink! The Shining Helmets won!

Folks, this has been another night of high-class hillbilly baseball! If you're heading home, check under your truck for stray dawgs, snakes, and squirrels. Keep your shine jars sealed tight, and remember: don't trust a man with clean overalls on game day!

This is CLETUS HOLLERBEE signing off for 89.5 POO-DUNK FM, where the static's strong and the stories are stronger! Now if you'll excuse me... HOOOO YEAH! I need a cold one and a long nap."

[06:30] – OUTRO MUSIC

(Banjo riff fades into buzzing static. One last hog squeal. Transmission clicks off.)

CHAPTER ELEVEN:

A HOT SATURDAY CONVERSATION — BOON AND ONE-EYE JACK

(Cicadas screaming in the heat. Screen door slams. A beer cracks open.)

BOON (grumbling happily):

"I tell ya what, One-Eye. Tippin' done gone full rogue. It's like that no-good cousin of ours who shows up uninvited to every fish fry. Parks his rusty truck right in the best spot, eats half the catfish before the blessing's even said, drinks up all the cold beer like it's his God-given right, then suddenly remembers he 'forgot his wallet' right when the check comes. Next thing you know, he's slinking out the back door with a to-go plate and half a pecan pie under his arm.

Now every cash register from here to Atlanta has a dang guilt trap bolted to it! You ain't just payin' for your sweet tea and boiled peanuts no more, brother. The gal at the Piggly eatery doesn't spin that tip screen around all slow and polite like she used to. Nah, she flips that thing like Aunt Vinnie after three glasses of sweet tea, a jar of moonshine, and a bad case of hiccups. Her arm goes windmilling, the screen smacks the counter, and suddenly, you're staring at suggested tips starting at twenty percent like it's the minimum bid at a charity auction for orphaned raccoons.

You just bought a pack of gum and a lottery ticket, and now you're getting judged harder than a Baptist church lady eyeing yoga pants on Sunday. Twenty percent? That's basically calling the cashier's kids ugly. Fifteen? Might as well spit on the floor and call her mama a possum. God forbid you hit 'No Tip'; that thing beeps like you just confessed to kicking a puppy on national television.

I swear, pretty soon they'll have tip screens at the funeral home. 'Would you like to leave a gratuity for the casket polisher? He did carry Uncle Skeeter the full twelve feet.'

Tippin' ain't service no more, One-Eye. It's a shakedown with extra cheese. And the worst part? I still tipped twenty percent at the Piggly Wiggly yesterday 'cause I ain't strong enough for that level of public shame. I'm weak, One-Eye. Before you know it, you're sittin' there, sweatin', hearin' an invisible voice that sounds suspiciously like your mama sayin', 'Mmm-hmm, you ain't really gonna hit "No Tip," are ya, sugar?' Next thing you know, you've just paid twenty percent extra 'cause the waitress handed you a sack of corn chips with a smile that said, 'You're goin' to hell if you don't be nice and tip me.' Shoot fire, I ain't ordering' a three-course meal! I just wanted gas-station nachos, not moral judgment!"

ONE-EYE JACK (snortin' beer, laughing as it comes out of his nose):

"Preach it, brother."

BOON (sitting back in a recliner):

"I'll tell you what. These fancy-pants city restaurants? Their 'suggested tip' starts at twenty percent! Twenty! That ain't a suggestion, that's ransom. It's like the menu says, 'Hey, we don't pay our folks nothin', so pony up, or we'll tell everyone you're tighter than Grandma's church shoes!'

Back in my day, ten percent meant 'you done good, darlin'.' It meant 'you refilled my tea before I dehydrated.' Now, if you don't cough up at least twenty percent, you're lookin' at judgmental stares from an iPad thing that thinks it's Saint Peter.

Don't even start on the self-checkouts! I had one blink at me the other day. The screen lit up all friendly: 'Would ya like to round that up to ninety cents?' I felt like cursin' as I yelled, 'For doin' your dang job?!' Then it sighed like an overworked waitress and started a vibrating hum like it was sayin', 'Guess not, Cheap-o.'

Buddy, the day I gotta tip a dang computer for lettin' me scan my own bag of chips and warm beer is the day I'm pourin' sweet tea straight into that USB port and callin' it a mercy killin'. I'm talkin' full rebellion. I'll hit 'No Tip' so hard the screen'll file for workers' comp. Keep this up, and pretty soon I'll be at the gas station pump arguing with a robot about whether filling my tank deserves hazard pay.

Heck, give it another year, and the dentist will finish drilling' a hole the size of a silver dollar, lean back, hold out his gloved hand, and say, 'That'll be a thirty percent tip for not hittin' a nerve. Don't forget the suggested gratuity for that numbing shot. That needle don't load itself!' I'll be lyin' there with cotton in my cheeks thinkin', 'I just paid you four hundred dollars to torture me with medieval tools, and now you want me to tip you for drillin' the wrong tooth? Next, he'll be askin' for five stars on the Yelp review while I'm still droolin' novocaine!'

I swear, tippin' culture done lost its ever-lovin' mind. It's gettin' so bad I'm thinkin' I'll start tippin' myself every time I survive another guilt-trip touchscreen without cryin' in public. Maybe we gotta push back, Jack. Maybe next time someone flips that screen around, smile really big and hand 'em a high-five instead of a dollar. Then tell 'em, 'You earned this spiritual tip, friend. You should feel good about it.' If enough of us do it, maybe we can start a movement. Call it 'The Tip-flation Rebellion.' Motto: Keep your change, keep your dignity, and don’t let a computer shame ya for likin’ your own money!”

ONE-EYE JACK (belching):

“Reckon that movement comes with beer?”

BOON (smiling as he continues):

“Well, now, two days ago, I picked up Ol’ Rusty from the groomer. He looked shifty-eyed and had this teeny, little doggone bow tie on him. He was lookin' like he's 'bout to go to church. The groomer hands me the leash and then spins that little screen around. It asks if I wanna tip. Five bucks for clippin' all four paws without getting’ bit. Ten dollars for gettin' rid of that rat's nest that was hangin' off Rusty’s ear. Twenty dollars for squeezin' him into that bandanna I never asked for! And wouldn't you know it, that dawg immediately sits up and offers the groomer a high-five! He looks at me like, ‘Come on, Pappy, don't be such a tightwad!’

I tell ya what, Jack, tippin’ done lost its ever-lovin’ mind. Used to be you tipped ‘cause someone earned it. They smiled, refilled your tea, and didn’t call you ‘honey’ with judgment in their eyes. Simple times. Now? It’s like everything has gone rogue, running’ around freelancin’ for the government. Every card reader from here to Tallahassee’s got its little guilt-trip program in it!

I went to the library, and the lady there wanted a tip of two dollars because she didn't shush anybody while I was there! When I hit that 'No' button, the lights flickered. I ain't jokin'. The whole building went dim. It was like the power grid itself was ashamed of me. Then that librarian just stared. Didn't say nothin'. Just gave me that librarian look—the kind that strips a man's self-worth quicker than a church gossip chain. She slid that book across the counter like she was handin' me my obituary and said, 'Enjoy your read.' Like she knew I wouldn't.

As I walked out, I swear those fluorescent bulbs hummed extra loud. It was like they were chantin', 'Cheap… cheap… cheap…' That's when I knew the truth: the tippin' plague is everywhere. Nobody's safe. Not even among the Dewey Decimals. Soon them book scanners will be sayin': 'Nice job savin' literacy, sugar! Tip 18% to keep libraries open. If you don't, the door will be locked!' At this rate, I'm expecting my preacher to pass the plate twice—once for Jesus, once for the service charge.

So, you know what I'm gonna do, Jack? I'm gonna start a rebellion. Free the people! We'll tip with high-fives and compliments instead of cash. Tell 'em, 'You done good, darlin'. The Lord and a stranger are both proud of ya.' The guy paying the wages needs to fork over the cash. Maybe someday, they'll remember it ain't about the money. It's about the heart. And also... about gettin' my dang change back."

(Boon takes a long drink, sighs)

"Now if you'll excuse me, I gotta figure out how to tip myself for finishin' this beer without throwin' my wallet in the creek."

Chapter Twelve:

The 47th Annual Possum Hollow Chili Cook-Off

It was hotter'n a bulldog's armpit on the Saturday of the 47th Annual Possum Hollow Chili Cook-Off—the kind of Georgia heat that makes the asphalt sweat and the gnats form organized militias.

Boon and Earl came rolling in like they owned the place. Every year, they are registered participants, always showing up with unshakable confidence and a cooler that looks like it has done hard time in prison.

Earl backed his dented-up Ford right up to the cooking field. The tailgate let out a long, pitiful squeal like it was begging for mercy as they wrestled out a cast-iron pot the size of a kiddie pool. Boon wiped the sweat from his brow with the back of his forearm and declared proudly, "This here chili's also known as Apocalypse Stew. One bowl'll either grow hair on your eyeballs or burn off everything you thought was hair down there. No refunds, no survivors."

Earl, who hasn't spoken a full sentence in public due to the trauma of living through the Obama administration, just gave a slow, solemn nod. He lifted a plastic milk jug full of something that smelled like a mix of kerosene, cough syrup, and horse liniment, pouring it into the pot without ceremony.

Boon looked around and said, "Some of this recipe came from the gold rush days in Georgia."

Nobody knew exactly what else went into that pot, but several eyewitnesses (all of whom later needed emergency medical attention) watched Boon dump in:

- Three pounds of venison that had been "aged" in the back of Earl's truck since deer season,
- Half a dozen peppers labeled "experimental nerve agent,"
- A mystery chunk of meat that was still actively twitching,
- One can of beer "for flavor," followed immediately by another "for hydration,"
- A suspicious amount of onions, beans, and enough extra 'maters to make the Baptist ladies clutch their pearls as they listened to the incoming gas rumble.

Local rumor has it that the recipe started as a bar bet in 2019. It involved a possibly haunted spice rack bought off Craigslist at 2:00 a.m. that required anyone within twenty feet to sign a notarized safety waiver. The fine print allegedly mentioned "possible spontaneous combustion."

By hour two, the fumes alone had cleared three square acres of mosquitoes, shaved the nose hairs clean off a Methodist deacon, and made a visiting vegan from Atlanta question every life choice that had led her to this field (the smell ultimately broke her spirit and made her eat a burger). Folks watching from a safe distance said they could tell the chili was ready when the pot started humming like a microwave full of forks. Steam rose in unnatural, neon colors as something deep inside gurgled like it was about to erupt.

The local fire marshal strolled up, took one sniff, quietly signed his life insurance beneficiary form right there on the hood of his truck, and walked away without a word. Right then, a confused possum fell out of a nearby pine tree, landed smack in the middle of the bubbling brew, and died instantly. Nobody fished it out.

Ultimately, they won the cook-off by default—mostly because all the other contestants ran for their lives.

Chapter Twelve and a Half:

Judging Time

(Boon and Earl don't like the number thirteen. They insisted there wouldn't be any)

When the three brave (or foolish) judges finally approached the table, Boon grinned like the devil handing out free samples at a tent revival.

Judge # 1, a retired barbecue legend from Valdosta, took one spoonful, turned the exact color of a ripe Cherokee tomato, and immediately began speaking fluent Latin. Nobody even knew he could do that.

Judge # 2 just stared into the bowl with wide, watering eyes, whispered, "It's… beautiful," and fainted face-first into the neighboring potato-salad bowl.

Judge # 3 managed to scribble the words "SEND HELP" in hot sauce on a paper napkin before attempting to baptize his entire tongue in a cooler full of Natty Light.

Someone in the crowd swore the chili whistled the first four notes of "Dixie." Someone else claimed it took the rust off a '72 Chevy hubcap in under thirty seconds. By the second round of tasting, the bowl had developed what local scientists could only describe as "conscious ambition… or a active death wish."

The Aftermath

Emergency crews stood by at a respectful distance with a garden hose. The local Catholic priest held an industrial case of Pepto-Bismol. The wind actually changed direction twice out of pure self-preservation.

One taster started levitating six inches off the ground. Another grew luxurious sideburns in under a minute while the hair on top of his head completely fell out. The line for the port-a-potties stretched clear into the next zip code and was described by witnesses as "a circle of Dante's Inferno that ain't on any map."

When the smoke finally cleared (and by "smoke" I mean actual rolling fire clouds that smelled like brimstone and cayenne), the head judge staggered forward. His eyebrows were entirely gone and his voice was hoarse.

"Boon and Earl… y'all don't get the Golden Ladle this year," he rasped, holding up a bright red extinguisher like it was a trophy. "But we are awarding you this here commemorative fire extinguisher and a lifetime ban from the chili cook-off!"

The crowd erupted into applause. A siren wailed in the distance. Boon took a theatrical bow. Earl gave one slow nod, still silent, and cracked open a fresh beer like it was holy water.

Boon hollered to the cheering masses, "We may not have won the ladle, but at least nobody died… yet!"

A paramedic wiping sweat from his face yelled back, "Check back in four hours!"

The next morning, Poo-Dunk woke up to find the scorched cast-iron pot still sitting dead center in the fairgrounds, quietly bubbling like it had unfinished business with the universe. Folks swear that if the wind is right on certain sticky summer nights, you can still catch a whiff of it coming in—part brimstone, and a whole lotta gas pains for everybody involved.

Somewhere out there, Boon and Earl nod, entirely satisfied with their dynamic version of a first, second, and third-place ribbon.

Chapter Fourteen:

Boon and Earl: A Right Good Mess

Boon slumped on Earl's porch swing, nursing a cheap beer and staring at a crumpled court summons like it was a death certificate. Their friends Stinker Jhon, One-Eye Jack, Cotton, and Cletus sat scattered around the porch with them.

"Earl, I swear on Dale Earnhardt's ghost, I'm fixin' to lose my license," Boon groaned. "And it's all on account of one power-trippin' deputy with a flashlight and a Napoleon complex the size of a Ford F-350."

Earl rocked methodically in his chair, chewing tobacco like it owed him money. "Spill it, Boon. What'd you do? Run over his favorite flowers?"

"Naw, man. Got pulled over doin' forty-two in a thirty-five..."

Earl let out a loud gasp for air. "Worth it! Frame that summons, hoss, and hang it right next to your 'Fish Shootin'' plaques."

"The only thing I'm drivin' now is this beer," Boon muttered, staring blankly at the can. "And maybe your golf cart, if you let me."

"Well, go get us some more beer then," Earl said with a shrug. "Keys are in the visor. Just don't tell the judge I aided and abetted a fugitive."

Boon walked off the porch with the heavy, dragging steps of a man who'd just lost his driving privileges. A few minutes later, he marched back up carrying a fresh six-pack like it was a trophy buck. They popped the tops and sat comfortably in silence for a minute, listening to the buzzing cicadas and the distant hoot of an owl that sounded like it was laughing right at them.

Earl broke the silence. "You know, all this talk about gettin' tackled and goin' to court reminds me of last turkey season."

Boon busted out laughing, the sting of his ticket momentarily forgotten. "Oh, Lord. I spent three weeks building the ultimate ghillie suit for that trip. Real moss, sticks, fake leaves, and enough burlap to outfit a small traveling circus. Looked like a walking swamp monster that had lost a vicious fight with a craft store. I looked right at Cotton and told him, 'This ain't hunting. This is becoming the turkey.'"

Cotton, who had been sipping coffee from a thermos and wearing normal camo like a sane person, just raised an eyebrow at the memory. "I told you right then, Boon—if you get shot, I'm telling everybody at the bait shop you died dressed like a haystack with commitment issues."

"We set up on a wooded ridge overlooking a creek bottom where the turkeys like to strut at dawn," Boon continued, gesturing with his beer. "We belly-crawled into position like special forces operators, then went perfectly still for forty-five minutes. I was so well hidden that a curious hen turkey actually walked right up and started pecking at the fake leaves on my back!"

"Cotton got excited," Earl chimed in, grinning. "Way too excited."

"He slowly tried to raise his shotgun to be stealthy, but the ghillie suit had other plans," Boon said. "One of my burlap sleeves caught on a root. Cotton yanked. The root yanked back. Suddenly, the entire creek bank gave way beneath us in a massive landslide of mud, leaves, and a rolling bottle of liquor! We tumbled down that slope like a deranged tumbleweed, picking up speed, sticks snapping, and fake feathers flying everywhere. Cotton was screaming words that would make a wild turkey blush. Halfway down, I hit a sapling that spun me like a pinwheel before launching me headfirst into the shallow creek."

Boon shook his head, laughing. "Cotton panicked. All he saw through the mud was a large, angry, feathery creature exploding out of the brush and thrashing in the water, making ungodly noises. He yelled, 'BEAR! Or... Bigfoot! Or demons!' and shouldered his gun. I surfaced from the muddy water just in time to see him aiming."

"COTTON, NO! IT'S ME—"

BOOM!

"Cotton shot high, thank God," Boon said, wiping his brow. "But the buckshot still absolutely shredded the top half of my ghillie suit that was floating on the water. Feathers and fake moss exploded into the air like a confetti cannon at a redneck wedding. I stood up in that knee-deep creek, dripping wet and half-naked, except for the remaining sad patches of burlap hanging off me like a rejected Muppet. A single turkey feather stuck straight up in my hair like a sad little flag of surrender."

From the porch, Cotton started wheezing just remembering it. "Best... hunt... ever! I lowered my gun, stared for a long second, and just had to sit down on the ridge because I was laughing so hard I couldn't breathe. Especially when that actual big tom turkey stepped out of the woods ten minutes later. It took one look at Boon's soaked, half-plucked, muddy disaster of a body, and let out the most judgmental gobble ever recorded in Georgia history. It sounded exactly like laughter. And there Boon was, water pouring out of his boots, flipping the turkey off with both hands. I got it all on video."

Ever since that day, Boon instituted a strict new rule: if the hunting gear weighs more than his hound dog, he's not wearing it. Furthermore, Cotton is no longer allowed to pick the hunting playlist—because apparently, "Tequila Makes Her Clothes Fall Off" is what Cotton blasts when he thinks he's tracking Bigfoot.

"I was lying there, soaked, half-frozen, covered in mud and my own shame," Boon laughed, clinking his beer against Earl's. "And all I could think was, 'Well, at least the deputy ain't here to give me a sobriety test.'"

Earl raised his can high. "To turkey hunters. May they never get organized. And to deer season, where the only thing gettin' shot at walks on four legs and don't talk back."

"Amen, brother," Boon said. "Now pass me another one before I start relivin' the time I got my boot stuck in a stump and wrestled a raccoon for twenty minutes."

Earl started to chuckle. "Oh Lord. The Great Raccoon Rodeo of 2024. Tell it right, Boon."

"So, I'm out behind the old barn tryin' to fix that broke fence line," Boon started, leaning back. "I was feeling pretty proud of myself that crisp autumn evening. I'd just finished chopping wood behind the cabin and stood there, axe on my shoulder, when I spotted it: a fat, masked bandit perched on the big old oak stump like it was his personal throne. I waved the axe for emphasis and yelled, 'Hey! Get off my stump, you trash gremlin!'"

"The raccoon—let's call him Bandit McTrash—tilted his head, gave me the slowest, most judgmental stare in raccoon history, and then did the unthinkable. He raised one tiny paw and flipped me clean off. At least, that's what it looked like to me."

"That was it. War was declared. I dropped the axe and charged like a caffeinated linebacker. The second my hands touched that coon, chaos achieved escape velocity. Bandit latched onto my shirt with all four sets of claws, and we went tumbling off the stump in a furious ball of fur, denim, and increasingly creative swearing. Words like 'Dad-Burn' and worse filled the afternoon air."

"We went rolling down the hill, through the leaf pile, clean across the pumpkin patch—RIP to three perfectly good pumpkins—and straight into the plastic kiddie pool I've been meaning to put away since September. Water exploded everywhere. I came up gasping for air with a plastic frog floatie stuck squarely on my head. Bandit surfaced right next to me like a Navy SEAL, shook himself once, and looked annoyingly dry."

"Round Two started immediately. I tried to grab the coon in a massive bear hug. Bad move. Raccoons are basically furry octopuses with severe anger issues. Bandit squirmed, twisted, and suddenly I was the one getting beaten up by something that weighed less than a Thanksgiving turkey. We rolled again, this time back up the hill in the opposite direction. Neighbors later swore they heard cartoonish 'booing' sound effects echoing through the trees."

"Finally, the fight returned to its natural habitat: the stump. We were absolutely covered in leaves, mud, and pumpkin guts when I made one last heroic lunge. That coon simply sidestepped like a tiny, furry matador, stuck out one back leg, and tripped me. I face-planted directly into the rough bark of the stump."

"For a moment, everything went perfectly still. Then that raccoon did something that will haunt my dreams forever. He sat right on the edge of the stump, looked down at me, and let out a noise that was unmistakably a laugh. Not a chitter. Not a hiss. A full-on, wheezy, evil little raccoon cackle—heh-heh-heh-heh—while holding his tiny paws to his belly as if he'd just heard the funniest joke in Poo-Dunk County."

"I lay there, cheek pressed against the bark, staring up at my new nemesis, and had to admit defeat. I said, 'You win this round, McTrash.' Bandit gave me a slow, regal nod—the true nod of a champion—and ran off into the woods, carrying one of my socks like a victory flag."

"The next morning," Boon grumbled, "I went outside and found the stump decorated with shiny beer bottle caps explicitly arranged in the shape of a middle finger."

Earl wiped tears of laughter from his eyes. "The best part of that whole deal was you smelling like a wet, wild animal for three whole days."

Boon raised his beer high again. "To raccoons, turkeys, and overzealous deputies..."

"Hold up now," Earl interrupted. "You can't talk about getting' humiliated by wildlife without bringin' up the Great Catfish Caper. That's the one that earned you the 'Fish Shootin'' plaque in the first place."

Boon groaned, though he was grinning under his breath. "Aw hell, I knew you'd drag that one out."

"Last summer, in the dead of night, we were out on the johnboat," Earl told the rest of the porch. "Engaged in what would quickly become the Great Catfish Catastrophe."

Boon took a long drink and took over the tale. "I swore this was going to be my absolute masterpiece. I told Cotton, 'The biggest flathead in the county lives right under that big cypress in the river. I can feel it in my bones, man. We are going to catch that monster.'"

"We launched the old johnboat at dusk—the one with the hull patch made from an old metal billboard beer sign. Cotton brought normal fishing rods. I, however, brought a rod thick as a broom handle, a trotline, a cast net, and my ultimate insurance policy: a .357 revolver, just in case we hooked a really big one. We tied off to the cypress tree and baited up with massive, stinking chunks of chicken liver."

"Everything was peaceful for about twenty minutes. Then I hooked something that felt like it had its own zip code. The fish turned into a submarine with a massive attitude problem. The heavy rod doubled completely over, the boat rocked violently, and suddenly this giant blue catfish broke the surface like a wet dinosaur, shaking its head and slapping the water hard enough to soak both of us."

"Boon, never one to play it safe, decided the best tactical move was to 'go in after him,'" Earl laughed.

"The boat flipped faster than a politician's promise," Boon admitted. "Next thing Cotton knew, he was treading water in the dark, watching me full-on wrestle a monster catfish in the river. It was a beautiful disaster. I put the fish in a tight headlock, and the catfish put me in one as we spun in circles. I yelled, 'I got him! I got him!' right before the catfish whipped its tail and smacked me square across the face."

"That's when things got biblical. I lost my grip. The fish started dragging me under like it had a personal vendetta. In full panic mode, I came up gasping, pulled the soaked .357 out of my waistband, and just started blasting wildly at the water!"

BOOM! BOOM! BOOM!

"Water geysers shot up everywhere!" Boon yelled, reenacting the scene. "Cotton was screaming, 'You're gonna shoot yourself in the eye!' while paddling away from me like an Olympic swimmer. Miraculously, one of the shots actually grazed the catfish or at least stunned it. I grabbed it again, wrestled it to the surface, and let out a victory yell that probably scared every living animal within three miles."

"The boat was completely upside down," Boon laughed. "The gear was floating halfway to Louisiana. There I was, standing chest-deep in the river, holding a massive, angry catfish like it was a heavyweight championship belt, bleeding from a few whisker punctures and grinning like a lunatic while a cottonmouth moccasin swam right past us. Cotton, clinging for dear life to the overturned boat, just shook his head."

"Technically... I caught it with modern technology," Boon reasoned. "We got the boat flipped back over—mostly by cussing at it until it complied—and paddled to shore with the giant catfish riding between us like a grumpy, oversized passenger. The outboard motor, of course, refused to start after its bath."

"The next morning, I showed up at the bait shop with the fish on a heavy stringer. By noon, Cotton had painted a brand-new sign on the side of my boat that read: Caution: May Discharge Firearm When Losing. Cotton claims it was the absolute last time he will ever step foot in a watercraft with me."

Boon raised his beer again. "To raccoons, turkeys, catfish, and overzealous deputies. May they all stay outta my way, or at least give me a fair fight and a good story to tell."

"Speakin' of things that blow up in your face," Earl chuckled, leaning forward. "You still ain't touched the Great Moonshine Disaster of last spring. That one nearly got our whole zip code condemned."

Boon put his head in his hands, groaning deeply. "Lord have mercy. Thankfully, I still have my eyebrows."

"Boon decided he was gonna cook up a batch of 'extra smooth' shine in that old copper still behind the shed," Earl explained to the guys. "Had it runnin' hotter than a two-dollar pistol. The pressure gauge looked sketchy from the jump, though."

"Here is how it went," Boon said, but Earl cut him off, yelling into the yard.

"Hey y'all, watch this, this here is science and chemistry!"

Boon snorted. "Science, my big butt. That thing started hissing like an angry bobcat trapped in a burlap sack. I was standin' right there with my mason jar ready when, BOOM, the whole apparatus erupted like a volcano full of boiling corn mash."

Earl was laughing so hard he was rocking the porch swing. "Mash and moonshine went everywhere! Looked like it was literally rainin' white lightning from the heavens. The whole backyard smelled like a commercial brewery caught fire. You came runnin' out of that thick black smoke cloud lookin' like a soot-covered chimney sweep, your hair standin' straight up, and your eyebrows completely singed off!"

"I was on fire! Literal fire!" Boon yelled. "Had to drop and roll around in the dirt like a prize hog while that still was spitting flames twenty feet into the air. Lost my best pair of overalls and dang near my manhood when a burning piece of hot copper landed right in my lap!"

Earl chuckled, wiping his eyes. "Then the smell hit the woods. Next thing we know, half the county's stray dogs, three raccoons, and one very confused deer come stumbling out of the tree line, acting drunker than hoot owls. A big ol' torn-ear raccoon even came back to the edge of the yard looking for seconds."

"We ended up puttin' the fire out with the garden hose and two cases of cheap beer," Boon sighed, shaking his head.

"Had to tear down the remains of the shed and tell the volunteer fire department it was a tragic barbecue accident. I still can't walk past that spot in the yard without smelling sour corn."

Earl let out a final, wheezy laugh, rocking his chair back. "The best part? The one solitary mason jar that survived that explosion tasted smoother than a politician's promise."

Chapter Fifteen:

Boon and Earl-The Neighborly Menace

Boon grumbled, taking a long pull from his mason jar and shifting uncomfortably on his wooden porch swing. "Yup, that boy up the hill is at it again."

Earl nodded slowly, whittling on a piece of wood. If there was one thing Earl had a genuine, god-given talent for, it was whittling.

"Yup," Boon muttered. "That young-un up the hill has a gift for causin' me grief. Earl, they say he was a gift to his momma when he was born." Boon scoffed loudly, spitting into the yard. "Gift? Seems to me he gets immense pleasure simply by annoyin' the ba-jeebers out of me! I gotta think of something, Earl. Something real good to get back at him. My blood pressure can't take much more of his tricks."

Earl didn't look up from his wood. "Like what did he do this time?"

Boon shook his head in absolute disbelief. "Well, first off, I thought the cat was dying. The poor thing was crappin' all over the place—mostly on my work boots, I might add. I was getting so worried about poor Mittens that I actually got out the shotgun to relieve its misery and put it out of its pain. But before I did anything rash, the wife stepped in and made me take the poor critter down to the vet."

Earl paused his whittling, lifting a single shaggy eyebrow. "Hmmmmm. And then?"

Boon threw his hands up in the air. "Cost me a whole chicken and twelve jars of my best homebrew just for the vet to check out a perfectly healthy cat! And now I find out the real reason for all the mess. That boy Jim-Boy up the hill has been sneaking over and poopin' directly in the cat's litter box! The cat stopped usin' it because Mittens has standards, Earl. Standards!"

Earl let out a quiet, raspy, shoulder-shaking chuckle. "Ha! Hee-hee."

Boon leaned forward, his voice dropping down to a conspiratorial whisper. "Oh, but it gets richer! You think that was bad? I just found out he put an ad in the Poo-Dunk Gazette advertising a massive garage sale at my house. And he wrote that it begins at 5:30 a.m. this Saturday."

Earl finally stopped whittling altogether, his eyes going wide. "Five-thirty in the morning? On a Saturday? That boy is a menace, Boon! He ain't just causin' grief; he's commitin' property theft by early bird special! You gonna have folks showin' up with flashlights before the rooster even thinks about crowing'. You'll have old ladies tryin' to buy the porch swing right out from under you before you've even had your first cup of coffee! You gotta put a stop to that, and you gotta do it fast. That young-un ain't right in the head. He's got the devil's own cunning, that one."

"Yep," Boon confirmed grimly. "He specifically wrote in the description: Priceless Antiques, Free Coffee, and The Owner is Motivated to Sell Everything Cheap."

Earl's face filled with genuine concern. "Boon, I think you're going to have a full-blown mob of bargain-hunting women here by dawn."

Boon ran a heavy hand over his face. "I know! I'm going to have to stand guard in my yard with a pitchfork! I swear, the only thing that boy won't try to sell is the dirt he stands on, and that's only because he hasn't figured out how to package it yet!"

Boon slammed his fist onto the porch railing, rattling his nearly empty moonshine jar. "All right, Earl. The kid wants to sell my stuff? We'll give him a yard sale he won't ever forget. This is what we're gonna do before the 5:30 a.m. fiasco hits. Here is the master plan:"

- The Sign Swap: "We're keeping the kid's original signs up. Yup, the ones pointing straight to my driveway. But we're adding a second, much bigger, highly confusing sign right underneath 'em. It'll read: FREE KITTENS! (Limit 5 per Customer, must present a valid Poo-Dunk Library Card). Nobody can resist a free kitten at 5:30 in the morning."
- Switch the Inventory: "We're going to put out exactly three things for the actual sale: A single, chipped porcelain doll named 'Agnes' dressed in a tiny, homemade parachute; one single old work boot—the one the cat didn't use as a toilet; and a massive, industrial-sized tub of expired mayonnaise. Oh, and I'm dragging out that old goat of mine that is so ancient it can hardly walk."
- The Payload: "I'm going to take that boy's favorite toybox from behind his shed. I'll fill it to the brim with hot molasses and about four pounds of pink glitter. It's the gift that keeps on giving. Then I'm rigging a small propane balloon inside with a trigger hooked to the lid. When he opens it, it'll pop and blow up right in his face. By the time the sun is up, Earl," Boon concluded with a triumphant, slightly manic grin, "that boy's going to spend his whole weekend cleaning sticky molasses and glitter out of his eyebrows, ears,

and other unmentionable crevices while I enjoy a hot, peaceful cup of coffee. Yup! What a plan!"

The next morning was thick and misty, and the faint, sweet smell of fermenting homebrew lingered in the air. The only illumination came from a sickly yellow porch bulb and the piercing high beams of a battered pickup truck that was idling its way to the very edge of Boon's gravel driveway.

Boon, wearing his absolute best pair of overalls, was slumped in a lawn chair next to his meager 'sale' items, gripping a garden hose like a weapon. Earl sat right next to him, sipping coffee from a thermos.

Earl nudged him. "Wake up, Boon! It's 5:28. I told you they would come early."

Suddenly, the pickup truck's engine gave a loud roar as the high beams swung across the yard, perfectly illuminating the premier inventory: a parachute-clad doll, a single work boot, and a massive tub of expired mayonnaise that even the farm goat refused to sniff.

A woman burst out of the truck cab, moving with the terrifying speed and determination of a professional linebacker. It was Brenda (better known around the township as Dit), the undisputed heavyweight champion of the Poo-Dunk early-bird bargain hunt. She was wearing a high-powered headlamp, a bright orange road-worker's safety vest, and a tactical backpack that looked sturdy enough for scaling Mount Everest.

Dit completely ignored the "FREE KITTENS!" sign and zeroed in on the porch. She skidded to a screeching halt right in front of the mayonnaise tub, panting slightly.

"5:30!" Dit shouted, consulting her glowing watch. "I'm on time! Where are the Priceless Antiques? The ad promised they'd be cheap!"

Boon slowly raised his garden hose nozzle, pointing it at the mayo. "That'd be that tub of Rare, Artisanal Spreading Cream right there, ma'am. Got to let it go for a measly sum of fifty dollars."

Brenda stared at the mayo tub. She leaned closer, her headlamp beam cutting through the morning mist and illuminating the blurry, unreadable expiration date stamped on the lid.

"Fifty dollars," she repeated flatly. Her eyes then darted to the lone boot. "What about this? Is this part of a matched set?"

"Nope," Boon said, shaking his head. "Just that one. But I tell you what, I will throw it in for free if you buy that tub of artisanal beauty cream."

Brenda's focus shifted to the creepy porcelain doll suspended by the tiny homemade parachute. "And what about that?"

"That's Agnes," Boon said, dead serious. "She's priceless. Frankly, it breaks my heart to let her go."

Dit took a step back, breathing heavily through her nose. "Is this it? I drove forty minutes through the dark for a single used boot, face cream, and a skydiving doll?"

Just then, a loud, raspy bleating noise erupted from the direction of the mailbox. Boon's ancient goat spotted Brenda's bright red backpack strap and immediately began a spirited attempt to consume it, dragging Jim-Boy's stolen toybox along behind it by a tangled rope.

Brenda yelped, jumping back. "What in Sam Hill is that?!"

Boon smiled a small, weary, yet triumphant smile. "That, ma'am, is the Real Early Bird Special. He's only two hundred dollars, and he comes with that custom toybox too. Better get him before the rest of the crowd shows up."

The goat gave a mighty yank on the bright red backpack strap, determined to make the nylon its morning snack, letting out a distressed, raspy, "MAAAAA!"

Brenda's eyes widened, and then, slowly, a huge, ecstatic smile spread across her face, blindingly illuminated by her own headlamp. "Two hundred dollars?! By the look of those teeth, that's an absolute steal! He really comes with that box, too?"

Boon blinked, momentarily thrown off by her immediate, unbridled enthusiasm.

"Well, sure, he comes with the box," Boon corrected himself hastily, pointing to the slightly dented toybox. "And, uh, the beauty cream will go with it too for forty dollars more."

Dit dug into her vest pocket and immediately pulled out a thick wad of crinkled green bills. "Done! Two hundred and fifty, not a penny more cash! And I'm taking the boot, too."

Boon and Earl exchanged a thoroughly bewildered glance over the hood of Brenda's truck.

"Five-forty in the morning, Earl," Boon mumbled under his breath as the truck door slammed shut. "And she's already bought me clean out."

Boon stared at the wad of cash in his hand, then at the empty patch of grass where his yard sale had been just a few minutes prior. "Well, Earl," he muttered, "I'm pretty sure she needs that beauty cream anyway. Look at her!"

The front yard fell oddly peaceful, except for the distant sound of Brenda's truck backfiring down the county road like it was celebrating a victory. All that was left behind was the smell of fresh woodsmoke, coffee, and the faint, sweet decay of expired mayonnaise that had somehow seeped through the plastic tub.

Earl calmly coiled the garden hose like a man who'd seen it all and was mildly impressed. "Yep," he said, wiping his nose on his sleeve. "This was some kind of yard sale. Thought I'd seen it all!"

Suddenly, a screen door slammed violently up the hill, followed by the unmistakable sound of furious stomping. Each step was heavier than the last, sounding like someone was actively trying to punish the earth itself.

"That's the boy from up the hill," Earl observed without looking up. "He's comin', and I bet he's about to crap himself."

Jim-Boy, the lanky teenage neighbor with perpetually messy hair and the smug expression of a failed mastermind, rounded the corner of the porch. He stopped dead in his tracks, surveying the empty yard. His eyes registered the vacant grass, the two old men casually sipping coffee, and the thick wad of bills resting in Boon's hand.

"What in the... where are the buyers?" Jim-Boy demanded, angrily adjusting his glasses. "It's six in the morning!"

Boon sighed contentedly. "Oh, we had a nice little turnout, son. Very enthusiastic buyers from all over town. Sold out everything."

Jim-Boy sputtered, his face turning red. "You sold it? What did you sell? Wait... where is my toybox?!"

Boon pointed calmly toward the gravel driveway where Dit had unhooked the rope. The morning sun had finally hit the box, turning the whole thing into a hilariously wrong science experiment. The molasses had warmed up to a slow, lazy ooze, dragging four pounds of hot pink glitter along for the ride. The mixture was dripping onto the gravel in a thick, sparkly stream that looked like a unicorn had eaten something rancid.

Jim-Boy approached the box like a man walking toward a live grenade labeled FREE CANDY. He reached out, hesitated—probably sensing his life was about to get 300% more fabulous—and poked the handle.

His finger came back looking like it had been dipped in a craft store's worst nightmare. There was a thick pink shimmer clinging desperately to a heavy layer of brown goo.

"What the heck is this?" Jim-Boy whispered, his face draining of color faster than a vampire at a garlic festival.

Suddenly—BANG!

The propane balloon inside gave up the ghost in spectacular fashion. A glittering, pink molasses tsunami exploded outward, nailing Jim-Boy square in the face like karma had hired a professional special-effects team.

"That, son of a dog-gone-dog," Boon roared, laughing so hard he spilled hot coffee onto his overalls, "is what goes around comin' around! Boy, welcome to the sparkly side of justice!"

Jim-Boy stared blankly at Boon, then at Earl, who was trying—and spectacularly failing—to keep a straight face behind his coffee mug. Earl's shoulders were shaking like he was having a private seizure, tears streaming down his weathered cheeks as he wheezed for breath.

"You glitter-bombed me!" Jim-Boy sputtered, his voice climbing from utter disbelief straight into full-rooster outrage. Pink goo dripped heavily from his eyebrows as if he'd just lost a cage match with a Bedazzler. "I'm gonna be finding this crap in my underwear for a week! It's in places God never intended glitter to go! That was low, Boon. Lower than your grandma's boobs!"

Boon took a slow, victorious sip of his coffee, his pinky finger extended like he was at a high-class tea party instead of a messy driveway.

"Low? Son, you got me to sell my whole junk pile this morning. I might add a thank-you for the extra cash, too. Reckon I'll buy myself a brand-new moonshine still with it. Or maybe just some industrial-strength Goo Gone and call it even."

Jim-Boy looked down at his sticky hands, then back up the hill toward his own house. "You haven't seen the last of me, Boon!" he bellowed, marching back uphill like a defeated glitter zombie, leaving a trail of sparkly molasses footprints that would stay embedded in Boon's yard for three seasons.

Boon waved lazily with his free hand. "Oh, I'm counting on it, son! Just next time, maybe I'll stick to somethin' sanitary for regular revenge. Hope you like dog poop, by the way. I saw your hound dog doing his patriotic duty right inside your left work boot this mornin'!"

Earl lost it completely, doubling over and cackling so hard his coffee sloshed right into his lap, screaming, "YEE-HAWW!" as Boon smiled.

"Well," Boon said, "just another peaceful morning in Poo-Dunk."

Chapter Sixteen:

Possum Poppers, Mud Bogs, and True Love

Earl sat with Boon in an old pair of rocking chairs, sipping a cold beer as he recalled the events of the previous week.

"Well, Boon, my Uncle Orvil, being the chief cook and bottle washer down at the mud bog fair, gave us a personal invite," Earl said. "Remember when we got there, and he cranked up that big propane burner and hollered, 'Y'all come get it!'? Shoot, everybody scattered like spooked quail. I ran LEFT, then hooked a quick RIGHT, then swerved LEFT again, all because I was tryin' to be first in line for them legendary possum poppers and that spicy deer chili."

Earl took a sip of beer. "Junior grabbed a couple of loaded paper plates and passed one RIGHT over to Tiffany. She took one teensy little bite, spun around on her heels, and upchucked RIGHT there on poor Aunt Linda's purty tie-dye skirt. Lord, have mercy! What an absolute mess!"

"After we stuffed ourselves, it was finally time for the annual mud bog," Earl continued. "Sammy just grinned at her and said, 'Baby, you gotta lay eyes on this! Hold my beer.' He hoisted Tiffany RIGHT up onto them bleachers—which was really just a three-story stack o' moldy hay bales pitched right next to the deep pit. First big truck roared its engine, mud went slinging twenty feet high, and one big ol' chunk of swamp muck nailed Tiffany smack in the middle of her face."

"She just wiped it off with her bare hand, flashed a big ol' one-tooth smile, and whooped, 'Now THAT'S what I'm talkin' about, ya'hear!'"

"Well, when the sun finally went down, Tiffany was caked head-to-toe in black mud, proudly holdin' a shiny trophy for Sammy. They call that trophy the 'butt picker'—the thing is great for picking up discarded cigarette butts and other trash out of the truck beds. Right then, Sammy knew he'd finally picked himself the RIGHT girl after all. Ain't that somethin'?"

"Then he proposed right there! Didn't even wait for her to finish the words 'yes, I'm saying yup.' Sammy's face was covered in a few stray specks of mud, split into a grin wide enough to show every single one of his three teeth. He let out a whoop that could rival a banshee on a coon hunt, throwing his hands high up in the air."

“He jumped up from the muddy ground, grabbin' Tiffany right by the waist and spinning her around until her muddy boots were kicking up dirt and hay dust. ‘Yes-sir-ee!’ he bellowed over the roar of the crowd, his voice cracking just a little bit with pure redneck excitement. He set her down, gave her a big, sloppy kiss right on the lips, and looked around at his family with the proudest look a man could ever muster.”

“Then, he grabbed her daddy's hand, shaking it like a rusty pump handle, and yelling, ‘We’re getting’ hitched, daddy! I got my house trailer's wheels off the blocks, too!’ He was so fired up he couldn't stand still, pacing back and forth, already planning the biggest mud-boggin' wedding reception this county had ever seen.”

Boon, having his priorities exactly right, drawled, “Hold my beer. I gotta pee.”

He handed his can off to Earl, who was far too busy trying to use a half-eaten corn dog as a microphone to notice, and Boon stumbled off into the bushes. The beer can slipped out of Earl's hand, fizzing and spitting into the dirt, adding a little extra flavor for the next round of boggin’. Yep, it was shaping up to be a perfect night.

When Boon returned from the woods, he wiped his hands on his denim overalls. “We gotta throw that boy a bachelor party.”

Earl let out a loud, "Yeehaw! Now we're talkin'! This ain't gonna be no fancy, city-slicker party with tiny sandwiches; this is gonna be a pure, legendary, down-home throw down."

The boys, led by Boon and a handful of second cousins, immediately started planning the party for Friday night, scheduled way out past the paved roads on Old Man Peabody's overgrown land. The itinerary was set:

- The Main Event (The Outhouse Blaze): The undisputed centerpiece of the evening was going to be the ritual burning of the old property outhouse—the exact one they swore they'd tear down last year. The plan was to soak it in five gallons of off-road diesel, light it up at midnight, and try to knock it completely over with a rusty old tractor before it burned down to ash.
- The Menu: They were going to cook a whole wild hog on a rotating spit over a massive fire pit dug specifically with a rented backhoe. Sides included fried taters, a heavy Low Country boil, a massive cooler full of ice-cold beer, and enough high-proof moonshine to strip the paint clean off a fleet of commercial dump trucks.
- The Mud Tire Rodeo: The boys planned a tire-rolling competition. They'd blindfold each fella, spin 'em around three times until they couldn't tell north from south, and make 'em push a massive mud-terrain tire back toward the starting line. The last one to make it

back had to drink a warm mug of beer spiked with actual deer pee.

- The Registry: Sammy wasn't getting any fancy city gifts like toasters, blenders, or matching towels. He was getting useful, practical gear: a brand-new heavy-duty tow strap, a motorized deer feeder, three cans of premium gun oil, four rolls of Gorilla duct tape, and a box of good, gently used spark plugs.
- The Grand Finale: The night would conclude with a traditional "shotgun salute" to the groom-to-be, where every single fella on the property would fire a live twelve-gauge round straight into the night sky, following the sacred, time-honored tradition of Poo-Dunk County.

The party was guaranteed to be louder than a straight-piped diesel engine on a freezing morning, and it was highly likely somebody was going to end up taking an involuntary mud bath, but it would be a memory worth tellin' for generations to come.

Meanwhile, Tiffany's friends, led by her plus-sized sister Brenda-Sue, were busy planning a bachelorette party down by the creek, making sure it had just the right blend of sweet femininity and rough-and-tumble mud-bog fun.

The girls were gonna set up a bunch of camo lawn chairs around a blazing bonfire, drinking sweet tea and maybe a little bit of spiked fruit punch. They planned to paint their fingernails bright, glittery colors and spend the night telling highly embarrassing stories about Tiffany's old high school days under the football bleachers.

Chapter Seventeen: Blind in One Eye, Blind in the Other

On Saturday morning, the bachelorette festivities kicked into high gear with a friendly competition down in the creek to see which of the girls could catch the most crayfish. The grand prize was a massive, shiny plastic crown.

Brenda-Sue had managed to borrow a souped-up, mud-tired four-wheeler, and the girls piled onto it to ride out to the local swimming hole, with Tiffany naturally claiming her rightful spot right up front. The dress code was strictly enforced: matching pink camouflage tank tops and sparkly shorts. Tiffany, the proud bride-to-be, topped off her ensemble with a custom veil fashioned out of a piece of old fishing net draped over her motorcycle helmet.

Down by the water, they played a high-stakes game of "Pin the Mud Spot on the Monster Truck" and held a rowdy tournament to see who could suck the most watermelon seeds straight up through a ten-foot length of green garden hose. They capped the afternoon off by cooking s'mores over the open fire and watching grainy, classic episodes of NASCAR on a portable, battery-powered TV, raising a sweet tea toast to Tiffany's big day. Lord, bless their cotton-pickin' hearts, it was a sight to behold. Everyone on the ridge knew the preacher was going to have to wear chest waders just to get through the ceremony.

By afternoon, the designated mud pit was steaming under the Georgia sun, decorated with flowing pink camouflage ribbons and featuring two massive tractor tires stacked up to serve as the altar. Uncle Josh, who had famously secured his minister's license online after failing the basic internet questionnaire seven consecutive times, was doing his absolute best to look official in his cleanest, least-stained denim overalls.

He cleared his throat and kicked off the service. "Howdy, y'all! Before we get started, can I get a collective 'yeehaw' for the bride and groom?"

The crowd unleashed a wave of drunken, engine-revving yells. Uncle Josh waited for the commotion to die down before continuing.

"Good. Now, if anyone here thinks these two shouldn't be hitched, you gotta speak up right now, or shut yer trap until the free beer tent opens up again." He paused, looking around the pit. "Alright, let's get this show on the road! Sammy the butt picker, why don't you tell this beautiful little kitten here why you're takin' her on as your permanent co-pilot?"

Sammy wiped a stray tear—and a fresh chunk of mud—from his eye. "Well, Tiff, when I first saw you upchucking on Aunt Linda's purty tie-dye shoes, I knew right then you was the one. You ain't scared of nothing'. You can out-drink, out-run, and most times, you smell alright. Plus, you look real nice today and make my heart do flip-flops. You're my kinda gal, baby. I vow always to save you the crow gizzards when we go hunting, always keep gas in the truck, and I will never, ever tell you to quit hollerin' at a good bog run. I love you more than fresh French fries or fried chicken, and that's the gospel truth!"

Uncle Josh nodded approvingly. "Amen! Tiffany, sugar, your turn. Keep it quick, though; we gotta hurry up because the next big-block truck heat is already waitin' at the starting line."

Tiffany adjusted her fishnet veil over her helmet. "Sammy, baby, I ain't got a whole lot to say, 'cause you already know it all. When that massive chunk o' swamp mud hit me square in the face from the bleachers, you didn't laugh at me. Well, you did a little bit, but you wiped it off for me. I promise to root for you when you're gettin' sideways in the pit, to keep your favorite cooler fully stocked, and to never overload the four-wheeler with my fat sister ever again. I wanna get stuck in the mud with you forever!"

Uncle Josh smiled widely. "Perfect. Sammy, you got the ring?"

Sammy fumbled around in his deep overalls pocket and pulled out a custom ring hammered out from an old eighteen-wheeler truck valve stem. "Yessir. Tiff, there ya go!" He proudly slid the heavy metal ring onto her finger.

"By the power invested in me by that internet license I finally printed out, I now pronounce you Man and Wife! Y'all can kiss, and then everybody get ready! Let's get out there and bog!"

Sammy and Tiffany shared a giant, sloppy, muddy kiss, and the crowd went absolutely wild, immediately cranking their loud V8 engines for the next race.

Later that weekend, One-Eye Jack came marching around the side of Boon's barn holding a brand-new, high-dollar fishing rod. It was no secret around Poo-Dunk that his wife, Linda, was thoroughly displeased about her butt cheek accidentally getting pierced by his rogue casting practice the day before. Needless to say, Jack's old fishing rod had been promptly snapped clean in half across her knee.

Linda slammed her hands right on her wide hips—the universal sign for a redneck woman fixin' to raise absolute Cain—and started squawking louder than a rooster at dawn.

"ONE-EYE JACK! You dang fool!" she yelled. "You come marching 'round here lookin' like the Grand Poobah of Bass Fishing, and you nearly put out your one good eye and hooked my hindquarters with your fishing junk! That ain't no way to treat a lady! You'd better take that dollar-store rod and put it away. That thing's worth more than the whole wedding layout yesterday. All you're gonna do is hook yourself!"

She shooed him off with a vicious wave of her hand, grabbed a stray can of beer Boon had dropped on the porch rail, and took a heavy swig. "Fool thinks money buys good manners," she grumbled, stomping off to find a rag to wipe down her purse, which closely resembled a small hardcover suitcase.

Boon watched from his lawn chair, shaking his head. "Oh, mercy sakes! You know high-falutin' gear like that four-hundred-dollar rod is bound to meet a tragic end in the hands of One-Eye Jack. He's blind in one eye and can't see out of the other."

Madder than a wet hornet after Linda's tongue-lashing, One-Eye Jack stomped right down to the creek. He arrived at his designated "secret spot"—which was really just a muddy bend in the river where everyone in the county dumped their old bald truck tires—and started fussing angrily with the high-tech reel.

He spent a good hour trying to cast it out, but the expensive pole was far too sensitive for his style. He couldn't feel any big, heavy lure; he was used to fishing with whatever rusted-up railroad spikes or heavy treble hooks he found rolling around the bottom of his tackle box. He kept snagging his line on the heavy briars, yanking violently, and at one point, successfully reeled a mossy truck tire completely out of the water.

Finally, he managed a mighty fine cast right into the deep channel. Feeling immensely proud of himself, he set the pole down on the bank for just a split second to light a cigarette. Unfortunately for Jack, he set it directly on top of a furious nest of fire ants. Within seconds, the ants were swarming up his legs, forcing him to shuck his pants completely off—right at the exact moment a massive alligator garfish hit the bait.

The fancy, high-tech rod bent completely double and shot off the muddy bank like a spooked jackrabbit, dragging the expensive reel right into the murky depths. One-Eye Jack yelled, leapt stark naked into the creek, but all he managed to catch was a face full of muddy water. He stood up in the current, dripping wet and angrier than ever, watching his four-hundred-dollar setup disappear completely out of sight down the river.

He walked back to the porch an hour later looking like a drowned rat, possessing nothing but a handful of minnows he'd managed to scoop up inside his underwear.

When Boon saw him walk into the yard, he took a slow sip of his beer and said, perfectly calm, "Well, Jack. Still lookin' for them fish fart bubbles?"

Meanwhile, Earl was sitting out on the porch swing, reading the latest edition of the Poo-Dunk Times. The front-page headline was screaming in bold black ink: LOCAL MAN IS BEAMED UP!

"Lord have mercy," Earl muttered. "They say a feller named Mr. Bob Hammer—just plain ol' Bammer to his buddies—done got sucked right up out of his own backyard. He was just trying to dig a little pond for his ducks when it happened!"

According to the article, Bammer told reporters that the very first thing them varmints from outer space did was pepper him with an interrogation about his backyard pig pen.

"They didn't give a coon's whisker 'bout no climate changes, or even how to make my secret barbecue sauce," Bammer explained to the press. "They purely and simply wanted to know why that dang ol' moonshine still of mine always stinks something' awful."

Bammer swore on a stack of Bibles that the aliens were exceptionally polite guests. They even offered to swap him a basket of fancy space mushrooms in exchange for the secret recipe to his famous Beet Rum. Bammer straight-up refused the intergalactic deal on account of strict family honor.

"Shoot, my daddy would come right up outta the ground and whoop my butt if I gave up the family recipe to a Martian!" he declared.

When the local deputies finally rolled up to the scene, they didn't release an official press statement, mostly because this wasn't exactly a case they wanted to log in the county books. They found poor old Bammer stark naked as a jaybird, wandering right underneath the big Piggly Wiggly sign town.

He was just a-wandering the parking lot, muttering and groaning about how tough life was way out yonder in the cosmos, going on and on about the heavy kick of those funny-looking space mushrooms the little green fellas had fed him.

He hollered at the deputies, "Them things weren't like the ones growin' under them cow patties down by the creek! They tasted just like warm bacon grease and made me see a giant black hole that looked exactly like a muddy hog wallow!"

Since nobody in the county had actually seen a spaceship, the Sheriff simply slapped a giant fluorescent sticker onto the final police report:

OFFICIAL DISCLAIMER:

The following statement may be the result of a close encounter of the third kind, too much cheap corn liquor, or them funny wild mushrooms growin' down by the creek swamp. Viewer discretion is heavily advised, and for the record, the Sheriff's Department ain't responsible for lost clothes, pond-digging' injuries, or citizens talking' to space critters.

Chapter Eighteen:

Hot Off the Poo-Dunk Press

The local law enforcement confirmed they had to drag a total of nine local shoppers out of the county Dollar General in handcuffs yesterday morning. High-ranking officials are calling it the wildest darn retail mess since the infamous "Great Candle War of 2001" at that very same location.

Witnesses reported that the pure, unadulterated chaos kicked off around 5:47 a.m. when the stockboys unveiled a massive clearance pallet of $3.99 steering wheel covers sporting official NASCAR branding. Lord, the morning crowd went absolutely hog-wild, surging forward like a whole herd of angry steers that had just consumed a fresh pot of high-octane coffee.

One local woman, bless her sweet heart, tried to hold her position at the front of the line by explicitly duct-taping her entire torso directly to the heavy metal shelving in the seasonal aisle. The responding deputies noted in their report that she was "mighty committed, but the maneuver still resulted in a total tactical failure."

Another feller was taken into immediate custody after he brandished a plastic fly swatter, swinging it wildly and threatening the responding officers.

The store manager, who was still visibly shaking like a leaf in a hurricane by mid-afternoon, reported that the automotive section looked like a high-speed demolition derby.

The Sheriff stated that the charges ranged from general disorderly conduct to flat-out "aggressive shopping and criminal abuse of retail goods." They noted that one frantic suspect even attempted to bribe the arresting officers, offering to hand over a fresh pack of tube socks if they would "just let him slide on the resisting arrest charge."

The responding deputy shook his head. "I swear, we ain't seen nothing' this crazy since the greased hog chase at the county fair. Folks were throwing left hooks and grabbing steering wheel covers like mad!"

Despite the corporate pandemonium, the head honchos at the Dollar General headquarters had to issue a public statement reminding patrons that "doorbuster deals are intended to be peaceful promotional events." (Which means, y'all, stop literally busting the front glass doors down!)

All in all, the great steering wheel cover blowout caused a hell of a lot more ruckus around town than the time a rogue barn squirrel shorted out Miss Patty's back-porch vibrator.

Chapter Nineteen:

The Canine Contender and the Sandwich Shop Citation

Stinker Jhon stopped by Boon's porch later that afternoon to grab a glass of sweet tea and deliver the latest local news. Boon, Earl, One-Eye Jack, and Miss Sue Ann sat back in their rockers to listen to the gossip.

First, Sue Ann clapped her hands together. “Lord have mercy, y’all! I swear on my grandaddy's prize-winning watermelon, you ain't gonna believe the sheer nerve of some people in this county. Yesterday morning, someone went and stole my brand-new steering wheel cover right out of my unlocked sedan!”

Suddenly, Sue Ann jumped up from her chair, running frantically toward the back yard. “Oh, honey, hold that thought until I pee! I gotta tell y’all the next piece of news, it'll make a farm goat laugh!”

In a short time, she was back on the porch, smoothing down her skirt, and One-Eye Jack took the floor to kick off his story.

"Well, listen up, 'cause this ain't no lie! Y'all know Bubba—he's got a head as hard as a chrome hubcap. He marched right up to Goofy's Sporting Goods yesterday looking like a hound dog that had just been chased off the porch by a pack of angry squirrels. His shirt was half-untucked, one work boot was completely unlaced, and he had that famous thousand-yard stare that says, 'I woke up mad at the world, and the world woke up madder at me.'"

"He was looking to buy a standard dog box for his coonhound, Duke the Destroyer, because Duke was currently turning the backseat of his extended-cab truck into a mobile flea circus. But Bubba, being Bubba, just stomped through the double doors mumbling under his breath like he was fixin' to fight the whole establishment."

"The teenage clerk behind the counter—a scrawny kid named Buster who still had way more facial zits than actual brain cells—perked right up. 'Howdy, sir! What can I help you with today?'"

"'I need a dog box,' Bubba growled, 'and make it a big 'un. Duke's been eatin' like he's trainin' for the heavyweight championship of the kibble world.'"

"Buster blinked twice, scratched his shaggy head, and lit up like a Christmas tree. 'Ohhh! You mean a boxing setup for your dog! Yes, sir, we got a full canine kit in stock. Gloves, protective headgear, even those little rubber mouthpieces so he doesn't accidentally chip a fang!'"

"Before Bubba could even say 'Bless your heart,' Buster was already dragging out a bright red pair of tiny boxing gloves with Velcro paw straps, a massive heavy punching bag that squeaked 'Ruff!' every time you hit it, and a dog-sized satin robe that read 'Duke The Drooler' in big, glittery silver letters."

"Bubba stood there, his mouth open wider than a catfish caught on a trotline. But you know how Bubba is—his stubbornness runs significantly deeper than a seed tick embedded in a coon dog's ear. Instead of correcting the kid and admitting he just wanted a plastic crate, he doubled down on his pride. 'Well hell,' Bubba muttered, 'if Duke's gonna keep fighting the mailman every Tuesday, he might as well learn how to train proper.'"

"Next thing you know, Bubba's walking out the front doors with seven hundred and eighty-seven dollars worth of professional canine boxing gear, a thoroughly confused but proud grin on his face, and absolutely zero dog boxes for his truck."

"That night, he rigged the heavy squeaking punching bag up to the back porch rafters and tried to teach Duke how to throw a proper left jab. Duke took one look at the setup, ate the red glove right off his paw, and then used Bubba's left shin as a chew toy. Now Bubba's walking around town with a fresh black eye, a massive bite mark on his leg, and a whole new level of respect for his hound. To top it all off, there is a viral video circulating on the local Poo-Dunk Facebook group right now titled 'Bubba's Hound Goes 12 Rounds with the Screen Door.'"

One-Eye Jack cracked open a fresh can of beer and kept the floor. "Now, on to other things."

"Y'all know Old Man Fitzwilliam, the one who's got that big commercial farm just past the Piggly Wiggly? Well, he woke up Tuesday mornin' and discovered one of the massive rear tires was completely gone from his big John Deere tractor. Not flat, mind you. Gone. Just a bare steel axle sitting miserably in the dirt."

"He called up Sheriff Bunnit, and Deputy Gladius came rolling up in the cruiser, scratching their heads in confusion. 'Fitzwilliam,' Bunnit drawled, 'that tractor tire weighs almost as much as my second ex-wife. How the blue blazes did somebody just walk off into the night with it?'"

"Fitzwilliam spits a big stream of tobacco juice into the weeds and says, 'I reckon they rolled it, Bunnit! You gotta find that thing fast! I need to plant my nuts!' Gladius looked absolutely shocked until Fitzwilliam clarified, 'I got a trailer full of seed peanuts that need to get in the ground today!'"

"So, the law spent the entire morning tracking that giant, heavy tire tread through the deep mud. The track went right past the general store, down by the creek bed, and finally stopped right behind Miss Ethel Mae's trailer."

One-Eye Jack took a long drink of beer and continued. "Turns out, Miss Ethel Mae—who is normally as sweet as a homemade peach pie but always has some crazy DIY project on the burner—decided her backyard garden desperately needed a brand-new retaining wall for her beefsteak tomatoes. She was just about to paint that big ol' John Deere tire bright white and fill it up with topsoil when the cruiser arrived! When Bunnit asked her why she went and stole it, she just batted her eyelashes real innocent-like and said, 'Steal? Why, I didn't steal nothin', Sheriff! The good Lord just rolled me a perfectly good planter right into my backyard!'"

"Bunnit just sighed, hung his head, and logged the whole incident as 'a minor misunderstanding of property lines and landscaping ethics.' We ain't had nothin' that exciting happen around here since the time the local raccoons broke into the church basement and got into the communion wine!"

One-Eye Jack sucked down the remainder of his beer with a loud sound resembling a shop-vac clearing out a clogged drain line, slammed the empty can onto the truck tailgate, and wiped his mouth with the back of his sleeve.

"Last but certainly not least," Jack said, his one good eye gleaming like a freshly polished marble in the sun. "Did y'all hear about Slick? Seems he was drivin' down County Road 4, arguing on his cell phone with his ex-wife about who gets custody of the Sears riding lawnmower, when a giant, prehistoric-looking possum crossed the asphalt right in front of his bumper."

"Now, Slick always prides himself on his lightning-fast reflexes—mostly developed from years of dodging his landlord—so instead of just tapping the brakes, he tries to swerve hard. In the process, he drops his phone, grabs his lukewarm cup of sweet tea by mistake, and slams his hand on the horn all at the exact same time."

"The final result: Slick didn't hit the possum. But he did manage to steer his '98 Chevy Silverado directly into the shallow end of Miller's duck pond at forty miles an hour."

"The truck hit the water with a massive splash that launched three local bullfrogs directly into low orbit. The engine coughed once, sputtered a thick cloud of black smoke, and died right there in the lily pads. Well, Slick sits there for a second, waist-deep in pond water inside his own cab, with a big piece of green duckweed stuck flat to his forehead. He picks up his phone—which was somehow miraculously still working—and looks out the driver's side window at the possum."

"The possum had just stopped on the grassy bank, turned around, and stared at Slick. It had its front paws crossed over its chest, looking down at the submerged Chevy like a thoroughly disappointed DMV driving instructor. It let out a long, slow, loud hiss, which Slick swears to God sounded exactly like, 'You can't park there, mate.'"

"To make a bad story significantly worse, his ex-wife was still on the line. When the truck hit the pond, his truck's Bluetooth speaker automatically cranked the volume up to maximum. Half the county could hear her screaming through the open windows: 'Slick? Slick! Did you just drive into that pond again? I told you not to talk on the phone and drive! I called to tell you I'm taking the weedwacker in the divorce too! I will call the tow truck again!'"

"By the time the commercial tow truck arrived, the possum had cleared out, but a family of local mallards had already nested on Slick's truck-bed toolbox. Slick was sitting cross-legged on the roof of the cab, fishing for his submerged work boots using a pair of jumper cables, trying to convince the tow truck driver that the entire incident was actually a 'tactical off-road maneuver.' Then the highway patrol arrived and handed him a hefty ticket for operating a mobile device while driving."

"Now, every single time Slick walks into Goofy's Sporting Goods, the boys behind the counter start making clicking and hissing noises, and somebody inevitably tosses a handful of stale white bread at his feet for the ducks."

Boon was right in the middle of a heavy rant about how the Georgia Bulldogs were going to absolutely crush it this upcoming season when Stinker Jhon's voice started yapping loudly on the speaker of Boon's phone, calling in from the road.

"Listen, y'all," Stinker Jhon drawled over the line, his voice crackling like overcooked fried chicken skin. "I'm starvin' like a prize hog at a vegan buffet. I'm gonna swing by that twenty-four-hour sandwich joint down the highway—the one with the glowing neon sub sign that looks like it's brown-eye winking right at ya."

Boon chuckled into the receiver. "You mean Subby's? Man, it's way after 9 p.m. Don't do nothin' stupid out there. Remember that old municipal city law on the books? There's no honkin' your horn at any establishment selling sandwiches or cold drinks after dark. The drive-thru workers will thank ya kindly for keeping the peace in that absolute slop hole."

Stinker Jhon snorted over the speaker. "Pfft, that's dumber than a screen door on a nuclear submarine. Who's gonna enforce that? The Sandwich Police? I'm pulling up into the lane right now—hey, the line here is longer than a politician's promise!"

Sure enough, the night drive-thru lane at Subby's was backed up with the usual late-night rush hour traffic. Stinker Jhon inched his truck forward, his stomach growling significantly louder than his exhaust pipe. Up ahead of him, some city yuppie in a shiny, polished SUV was taking an absolute eternity, aggressively arguing with the speaker box about getting extra pickles on his wrap.

Jhon's fragile patience snapped like a brittle pretzel. Without thinking, he leaned his heavy forearm right onto his horn.

BEEEEEPPPP!

The massive blare echoed through the quiet night, scaring a whole flock of resting pigeons clean off the restaurant roof and making the drive-thru speaker feedback sound like a terrible karaoke night.

Boon yelled into his phone, "Jhon, you total idiot! What'd you just do?!"

Before Jhon could even offer a response, bright blue police lights started flashing violently in his rearview mirror. Out of the cruiser stepped Officer Gladys, a no-nonsense county cop who'd been patrolling the roads of Poo-Dunk since the dinosaurs roamed the earth. She sauntered up to the truck window, ticket book already in hand, her silver badge glinting under the flashing neon sub sign.

"Sir," Gladys said, peering into the cab with a glare that could easily curdle sour milk, "did you just honk your horn at this establishment after nine o'clock in the evening? This here is a verified sandwich shop selling cold beverages. That is a direct violation of city ordinance. The citizens of this township demand quiet after dark, so you're gettin' heavily fined."

Stinker Jhon's jaw dropped. "You gotta be kidding me, Officer! It was just one little accidental honk because the guy ahead of me was stalling!" Holding up his glowing phone toward the window, he pleaded, "Boon, tell her! Boon?!"

Boon, laughing hysterically on the speaker, chimed in, "We are completely deaf, Officer, can you please repeat that for the record?" Boon then chuckled at his buddy. "I told ya, Stinker! Don't you know the rest of that old code? Any man who flirts with, makes goo-goo eyes at, or winks at any female person on the public streets can be legally arrested!"

Officer Gladys smiled like a prize hog that had just uncovered a massive bucket of corn, then reached directly for her handcuffs.

Jhon spent the remainder of his evening eating cold french fries in absolute silence down at the county police station, paying a cool one-hundred-and-fifty-dollar fine for his impatience. From that night on, whenever Stinker Jhon drove past Subby's after dark, he'd wave frantically out his window at the cars ahead of him, looking exactly like some kind of deranged, silent mime. Officer Gladys keeps a real close eye on Stinker Jhon now.

Boon leaned back in his porch rocker, wiping a tear of laughter from his eyes. "Well, y'all, just another peaceful morning in Poo-Dunk."

Chapter Twenty:

The Chicken Fork Creek Blues

Two locals from Poo-Dunk recently took a trip up to Gainesville, the poultry capital of Georgia, where they learned some of the state's wildest laws. By the time they got back, the sun was a mean, yellow eye hanging low over Chicken Fork Creek, casting long shadows across a rusty road sign by the bridge that warned in bold letters: NO FORKS ALLOWED WITH FRIED CHICKEN.

It was a literal, official city ordinance in Gainesville, and although Chillin' Edger and Fishin' Charlie had never actually seen it enforced by a swat team, they certainly weren't about to become the county's first test cases.

Fishin' Charlie, a man whose weathered face looked like a well-worn catcher's mitt and who smelled permanently of industrial-strength bug spray, was sitting flat on the tailgate of his rusty pickup truck, plucking a mournful tune on his banjo. Beside him sat Chillin' Edger, whose nickname came from the fact that he was currently lounging inside a velvet-lined casket he'd pulled out of his barn and repurposed into a patio chair.

“Edger,” Charlie drawled, his straw hat tipped low over his eyes, “I'm gettin' mighty worried 'bout this here llama.”

“That ain't no llama, Charlie. That’s a mule,” Edger replied, refusing to move a single muscle.

“Well, whatever it is,” Charlie insisted, pointing his fiberglass fishing rod at a woolly, thoroughly confused-looking creature standing near a tree where a cardboard sign clearly stated: DON’T FEED THE DAD-GUM THING.

“Sheesh, Charlie,” Edger sighed, sitting up slightly in his casket. “First off, that’s a llama. I won her fair and square in a high-stakes poker game last month. And second, the feller who lost the hand explicitly said it was a llama.”

Fishin' Charlie pointed his rod again, this time zeroing in on a scrawny white chicken nervously pecking at the gravel road. “It's crossing', Edger! The chicken is actively crossing the road!” Charlie burst out, his voice climbing an octave. “It's illegal, man! A chicken cannot legally cross the road here in town! We're gonna be booked as accessories to a poultry crime!”

“Oh, Lord. Here we go again,” Edger mumbled, rolling his eyes.

Suddenly, a booming voice echoed from the creek bank. “Watch your mouth, Charlie!”

The two men froze. A local named Billy-Ray was bent over a pile of dry leaves near the edge of the property line. He was clutching a heavy garden rake—a mandatory tool in these parts according to Acworth's civic ordinance, which stated every single household head was legally required to own a rake.

"Billy-Ray, you know the rules," Edger said sternly, pointing a finger from his casket. "You cain't go hollerin' near dead people! Or things that look like dead people. The neighbors get upset when they hear yelling near a coffin."

"But I ain't said nothin' bad! I just said, 'Shoot-Fire!'" Billy-Ray protested, defending his honor.

"Don't matter! It's all about the context! Now, shut yer trap and let me chill." Edger settled back down into the velvet, covering his face with his straw hat.

Charlie just shook his head, let out a heavy sigh, and went right back to strumming his banjo. He began to croon the words to a brand-new tune right there on the tailgate. "A llama, a donkey in a tub, a coffin, and a potentially criminal chicken. It was just another peaceful afternoon on Chicken Fork Creek."

Together, their voices blended over the water:

(Both singing)

Oh, the Chicken Fork Creek Blues done got us in a bind,

Tryna keep the peace with the craziest laws we find.

Donkey in the bathtub, the corpse ain't likin' no sound,

And if we eat this chicken, we can't let a fork be found!

It's against the law!

(Verse 2 - Charlie strumming)

Chillin' Edger stretches out, lets out a heavy shock,

Heard Billy-Ray yell "Shoot!" and nearly fell right off the block.

"Charlie, that ain't a corpse, it's just my nap-time lounger,

But if you cuss near me, son, you're gonna feel the danger!"

Hand me a fried drumstick, boy, but keep your fingers bare,

If you use a silver utensil, the Sheriff will lock you up in there!

(Chorus - Both roaring)

Oh, the Chicken Fork Creek Blues done got us in a bind,

Trying to keep the peace with the craziest laws we find.

Donkey in the bathtub, the corpse ain't makin' a sound,

And if we eat this chicken, we can't let a fork be found!

(Charlie solo)

The llama looks at the donkey, the donkey looks at the tub,

I'm lookin' at that criminal chicken, wonderin' 'bout the law that says it ain't allowed to cross the road for grub...

(Outro)

So Edger hits a high note, Charlie hits the strings,

Just two good ol' boys dealing with the trouble that life brings.

The llama spits, the chicken runs, the donkey gives a grin,

It's just another peaceful afternoon...

(Fade out)

...That is, 'til the Sheriff pulls in!

CHAPTER TWENTY-ONE:

EARL'S COOLED COMFORT

Earl Ray had exactly two true loves in this world: his rusty, four-wheel-drive Ford Ranger and anything that involved a healthy, excessive dose of industrial super glue.

It was now the third week of August in Poo-Dunk County, and the local heat index had officially hit a record level best described as "Melted Butter on a Hot Grill." Earl's ancient window air conditioning unit, bless its tired soul, finally gave up the ghost with a terminal screech that sounded like a feral cat trapped inside a spinning washing machine.

Now, Earl didn't have any actual cash on hand to buy a replacement unit, but he did possess a boatload of pure backwoods ingenuity. After wiping the dripping sweat from his brow, he looked from the busted AC unit hanging out his trailer window to the large, deep-chest freezer he kept plugged in on the back porch for his winter deer meat. A metaphorical light bulb practically shattered the air above his camouflage hat.

He hauled the massive freezer onto the porch. Using a handheld jigsaw, he carefully cut a perfectly square hole in the back of the appliance and another matching square hole directly through the exterior wall of his living room. He sealed the entire perimeter with a generous, airtight application of silver duct tape and roofing tar.

Next, he found an old three-speed box fan and bolted it right over the opening inside the freezer cavity. He loaded the appliance with fifty pounds of cubed ice and plugged the whole contraption in.

The box fan immediately sucked the frigid air from the ice-filled chamber, pushed it through the wall, and blasted a glorious, sub-zero Arctic gale straight into Earl Ray's living room. It worked like an absolute charm! Within twenty minutes, the room temperature dropped to a beautiful 65 degrees.

Earl leaned back in his vinyl recliner, took a long sip of his sweet iced tea, and watched the NASCAR race in total comfort. "Them high-falutin' mechanical engineers in Detroit got absolutely nothin' on a redneck with a chest freezer and a fresh roll of silver tape," he muttered happily, as the soothing hum of his new Arctic Blast Air Conditioner lulled him toward a deep afternoon nap.

The setup was absolutely flawless—right up until a family of local raccoons decided that the thawing deer meat inside the freezer would make an excellent weekend buffet. Those pesky masked bandits smelled the meat from a mile away, drawn by the scent escaping into the heat.

Earl Ray woke up to the box fan making a terrible, clattering racket, accompanied by a whole lot of aggressive scratching. He jumped out of his chair, threw open the trailer door, and lifted the freezer lid. There stood three fat raccoons, casually having a full buffet right next to the spinning fan blades!

One of the coons was sitting directly on a block of ice, looking up at Earl with an expression that clearly said, "Hey, thanks for the air conditioning, buddy!"

Earl didn't even bother to yell. He just marched to the yard and went straight for the garden hose. He thoroughly soaked those raccoons with a high-pressure stream, slammed the heavy freezer lid shut, sealed it down with two additional layers of silver duct tape, and wrapped a heavy-duty bungee cord around the entire perimeter for good measure.

"Well, I reckon this here appliance is now a certified, Coon-Proof Arctic Blast A/C!" he declared triumphantly to the empty yard. It wasn't official, but he was willing to bet every single trailer house on the ridge needed an Earl Ray original cooling system.

Chapter Twenty-Two:

The Gas-Guzzling Genius

Following the roaring success of his home cooling system, Earl Ray decided to invent a custom window air conditioner specifically for the back glass of pickup trucks. The primary engineering obstacle, however, was keeping gasoline in the portable generator required to power it in the truck bed.

First, he grabbed a couple of cheap box fans—the kind you buy for three bucks at a neighborhood yard sale—and rigged them up with a generous amount of silver duct tape directly over the rear windows of his Ford Ranger. The fans stuck out sideways at an odd angle, making the truck look like it was wearing a pair of giant Mickey Mouse ears.

The truly ingenious part of the layout involved the actual window AC unit from his trailer. He mounted the heavy appliance onto a wooden shipping pallet and used a literal mountain of plastic zip ties to secure it right next to a sputtering gas generator sitting in the bed of his truck. He ran the primary cooling vent directly through the sliding back glass window of the cab. It pumped pure, ice-cold air straight down the driver's neck. It was absolute glory!

There was only one problem: that big generator drank gasoline like a thirsty camel drinks water after a month in the Sahara Desert. Earl Ray would pull out of his gravel driveway feeling as cool as a cucumber in a snowbank, but he'd get maybe ten miles down the county highway before the generator would cough, sputter, and quit. The AC would instantly die, and that glorious cold air would turn into the suffocating stink of burnt motor oil in about five seconds flat.

He'd have to pull over onto the shoulder, pop the cap on his main truck tank, and manually siphon a gallon of fuel out of the truck's tank directly into the generator's tiny little plastic reservoir. Every single time, he'd end up spitting gas onto the asphalt, coughing, and saying, "Durn it, you thirsty little bugger."

He spent significantly more time pulled over on the side of the road sucking fuel out of his own vehicle than he did actually driving the truck. By the time he completed a simple ride to Brenda-Sue's house to pick up some extra ice bags, he had to stop six separate times just to feed the generator. Still, in his mind, he had successfully engineered the cheapest replacement cooling system in the state.

Boon, his best friend, just shook his head in absolute disbelief when he saw the contraption idling in the yard. "Earl Ray, you know you already got a factory-installed two-forty air conditioner built right into that truck, right? Just roll down both windows and do forty miles per hour!"

Chapter Twenty-Three: Park, Throttle, and No Reverse

Earl Ray was never the sharpest cracker in the box. Shoot, truth be told, he wasn't even the cracker that successfully made it into the box during production. He was the misshapen one that fell onto the factory floor, got stepped on a few times by the night shift, and was finally swept into the dusty corner behind the breakroom stove along with the dead flies and lost buttons.

If you ever asked Earl Ray a complicated question—something with more than one moving part, like "How do taxes work?" or "Why do you reckon the neighbor's cows keep gettin' into our garden?"—you could watch his entire mental processing system happen in real time. His eyes would drift off in two completely different directions, his mouth would hang open just enough to let a little ambient air in, and he'd scratch at the thick stubble on his chin like he was trying to physically spark an idea out of his jawbone.

After a few seconds of agonizing silence, you'd finally hear it: a faint, metallic whirring sound deep inside his skull, sounding exactly like an old Briggs & Stratton lawnmower engine that had been sitting uncovered out in the winter rain since Thanksgiving. That was Earl Ray's brain trying to find the gear labeled "Understanding." Most of the time, the clutch just spun, smoked, and eventually gave up entirely.

But Lord help us, the one thing that rusty little mental motor was exceptionally good at was finding a shortcut.

Earl Ray couldn't tell you the first thing about advanced calculus, physics, or why the sky is blue, but he could successfully bypass every single factory safety feature on a heavy piece of machinery with nothing but a piece of an old wire coat hanger, a rusty ball-peen hammer, and half a case of lukewarm beer. He approached mechanical engineering the exact same way a raccoon approaches a suburban trash can: with a sense of pure, opportunistic brilliance mixed with a total, joyous disregard for future consequences.

Give him a riding lawnmower that hadn't run since the Clinton administration, and five minutes later he'd have it running wide open down the road with no governor, no kill switch, and a custom throttle rigged directly to the choke lever using a piece of rusty baling wire.

Bless his peanut-pickin' heart, the boy possessed raw survival instincts right where his common sense was supposed to live. If he ever got lost in the woods (which happened far more often than you'd think for a man born and raised in the exact same zip code), he didn't bother looking for a map or reading road signs. He'd simply roll his truck window down, sniff the morning air like a prize coonhound, and steer the truck in whatever direction smelled like something was currently frying. Fried chicken, fried catfish, fried okra—it didn't matter.

Strangely enough, it usually worked. More than once, he'd end up at his destination, grinning wide to show his gap-toothed smile as if he'd just solved a Rubik's Cube, covered in grease, telling a long story about how the afternoon wind had carried the scent of Miss Eula's fried chicken livers straight to his nose.

Some folks called it dumb luck. Earl Ray called it "God-given talent."

Take the time his brother-in-law, Dwayne, asked him to look at an old Ford tractor that had been sitting behind the equipment barn for three solid years, collecting rust and bird nests. The engine wouldn't crank, the drum brakes were completely seized, and the main PTO shaft looked like it had been aggressively gnawed on by a family of radioactive beavers. Most folks with half a brain would've hauled the wreckage straight to the John Deere dealer or the scrap yard. Not Earl Ray.

He disappeared into the dark tool shed for about forty-five minutes with nothing but a basic socket set, a can of starting fluid, and a six-pack of beer. When he finally hollered, "She's ready!" the whole family marched out to the yard to watch the disaster unfold.

Earl Ray climbed up onto the metal seat, twisted the bare ignition wires together, and that old Ford tractor roared to life with a thunderous backfire as if it had just been born again. The problem was, he'd completely hot-wired the ignition, entirely bypassed the neutral safety switch, and somehow rigged the throttle link so it only possessed two settings: idle and "run like the devil himself is chasing you."

Dwayne took one look at the vibrating machine and said, "Earl Ray, that thing ain't got no working brakes, and you completely removed the reverse gear. How the hell am I supposed to use it?"

Earl Ray just grinned, wiped his greasy hands on his already filthy overalls, and shrugged his shoulders. "Park and throttle, brother. That's all a real man needs in this life. You just point her exactly where you want to go and commit to the ride. If you need to stop, you just cut the key wire and jump off fast into the grass. Works every single time."

That tractor became an absolute legend across three counties. Locals started calling it "Earl Ray's Suicide Sled." It mowed overgrown cattle pastures significantly faster than anything equipped with a proper transmission, but it also successfully took out two fence posts, one brick mailbox, and nearly Dwayne's prize breeding boar before they finally managed to chain the machine to a live oak tree to stop it. Every single time someone brought up the machine down at the feed store, Earl Ray would lean back against the counter, crack open a fresh beer, and proudly declare, "See? Shortcuts ain't about being lazy, boys. They're about being efficient, easy, and simple."

Of course, not all of his bright ideas ended in a victory lap. There was the summer he decided the family riding lawnmower desperately needed "more giddy-up." After an afternoon of creative rewiring and successfully bolting a much larger commercial motor onto the small chassis, he managed to make the mower clock forty miles an hour across the backyard. The kids thought it was the greatest invention since sliced bread, right up until Earl Ray hit the hidden irrigation ditch at full speed.

The lawnmower went completely airborne, flipped twice in the sky, and landed upside down in the middle of the duck pond. Earl Ray came walking out of the muddy water a minute later, soaked to the bone, covered head-to-toe in green duckweed, still proudly holding the detached steering wheel like a trophy.

His wife, Darlene, stood on the back porch with her hands locked tightly on her hips and hollered, "Earl Ray, have you completely lost that little bit of mind the good Lord gave you?!"

He just spit out a mouthful of murky pond water, flashed that gap-toothed grin of his, and said, "Darlin', I was just testing the flight characteristics of the deck. Next weekend I'm adding wings."

Darlene just shook her head in despair, muttered something about checking their life insurance policy, and went back inside to finish frying supper. But deep down in her heart, she knew the truth: Earl Ray might not have been blessed with standard book smarts, but he possessed a kind of fearless, backwoods ingenuity that kept life interesting. Dangerous as all get-out, sure, but never boring.

Nobody understood this raw philosophy better than his Uncle Roscoe, the wild-eyed, tobacco-chewing human tornado who had poured most of that fearless ingenuity straight into Earl Ray's skull since the boy was old enough to hold a crescent wrench. Roscoe was sixty-eight years old, skinny as a fence rail, and was never seen in public without his faded red "Kiss My Bass" baseball cap and a grey beard that looked like it had been used to clean chimneys for a living. He was fully convinced the federal government was actively slipping mind-control drugs into commercial chewing gum (which is why he stuck strictly to raw leaf tobacco) and believed that every factory-installed safety shield was a personal insult from "city boys who ain't never bled on a rusty bolt."

Roscoe had been Earl Ray's hero, teacher, and occasional partner in near-fatal disasters for decades. It was Roscoe who originally taught him that "if a project ain't trying to kill you at least once during construction, you ain't doing it right." It was Roscoe who showed up one blistering July afternoon when Earl Ray was nineteen, towing a doorless 1972 Chevy Blazer he swore he'd won in a midnight poker game against a one-eyed bootlegger in Valdosta.

"Time for your graduate degree, boy," Roscoe had rasped, spitting a brown stream of juice into the dirt yard. "We're gonna set this machine free."

For the next six hours, the two of them worked under the shade of a pecan tree, surrounded by empty beer cans, cut-up exhaust pipes, and enough baling wire to stretch completely to the county line. Roscoe removed the catalytic converter with a reciprocating saw—"so she can properly breathe," he explained—drilled twenty extra holes straight through the air cleaner lid—"so the engine can holler at the neighbors"—and swapped the factory steering wheel for a tiny plastic one he'd yanked off an old Sears riding mower.

When they finally cranked the ignition, the Blazer roared like a mythical dragon and shook so violently that the milk-crate seats rattled like dice in a cup. Roscoe climbed into the driver's side, gave Earl Ray that wild, gap-toothed grin, and declared, "Park, throttle, and no reverse, nephew. That's the Holy Trinity of real driving."

He stomped the gas pedal. The Blazer launched forward in a massive rooster tail of gravel, plowed straight through Darlene's prize rose bushes, and disappeared down the dirt road in a cloud of thick black smoke and pure glory. Three hours later, Uncle Roscoe came walking back up the driveway alone, sporting a fresh black eye and absolutely no Chevy Blazer.

"The tree won," was all the explanation he offered, before grinning like a man who'd just won the state lottery.

Since the day Roscoe passed away, every single time Earl Ray rigged up something highly dangerous on the porch, he could hear his uncle's raspy voice whispering in the back of his mind: "She'll hold, probably. Give 'er hell, boy. You have to live large and keep life exciting."

And that, more than anything, was what lived inside Earl Ray's head: a wild, half-baked carnival of half-finished ideas, bypassed warning labels, disconnected safety switches, and the constant echo of Uncle Roscoe cackling somewhere in the distance. It was an unshakable belief that if you just kept turning wrenches, following the smell of fried food, and occasionally tempting fate, everything would turn out just fine. Dangerous as all get-out, but never, ever boring.

CHAPTER TWENTY-FOUR:

'BOUT BOON

Let me tell ya, Boon is the craziest, hardest-working son-of-a-gun ever to sling mud in the holler of Poo-Dunk!

Now, most folks around these parts look like they've been actively wrestled by a John Deere tractor and lost every single round. They've got skin like old boot leather, backs permanently bent from hauling square hay bales, and hands so calloused they could easily sand a two-by-four smooth without sandpaper. But Boon? He's a farmer, sure enough—growing corn, beans, and enough okra to feed three entire counties—but he's different. The man's got these eerie, glowing blue eyes that could spot a seed tick on a squirrel's tail from a mile away. Locals swear those eyes glow significantly brighter when the moon is full, like God gave him built-in high beams for the soul.

From sunup to sundown, Boon can plow a perfectly straight furrow across forty acres of rough Georgia clay, fueled by nothing but sweet iced tea and a bowl of breakfast grits so thick you could stand a metal spoon straight up in 'em. He'd sing classic Hank Williams songs to his mule, talk to his tractor engine like it was his absolute best friend, and still finish a fourteen-hour day with a grin wider than the creek after a summer gully-washer.

But where Boon truly shines is after the sun dips completely behind the pine ridge. That's when the real backwoods magic happens.

Most men in the county fish with worms, crickets, or store-bought stink bait that smells like a landfill. Not Boon. Naw, this feller's secret weapon was a handful of ripe raspberries he'd picked fresh from the briar patch that afternoon. He'd settle down on the muddy creek bank at dusk with a mason jar, a sack of berries, and a cane pole that looked older than Moses. He'd drop one fat, ripe raspberry into the dark current every so often and wait.

Before long, the channel catfish would start leaping clean out of the water like they were auditioning for a traveling circus, fighting each other aggressively just to get to that sweet berry goodness. Boon always claimed it was because "catfish got a sweet tooth just like the rest of us humans." Nobody in town could argue with the results; he'd walk back into his kitchen before dawn with a stringer of fish so heavy that it literally dragged the ground behind him.

Now, Boon's personal philosophy has always been simple: You Gotta Feed Your Fat. You gotta have a steady diet of fresh catfish, hush puppies, hot grease, and heavy grits that'll properly feed the soul! Even the old, stubborn coots sitting down at the Poo-Dunk VFW have started nodding along in agreement with his cooking rules.

Folks around Poo-Dunk still talk about his brief town campaign with a wide grin. Every single time a local complains about the lack of decent fried food choices or the sorry state of local entertainment options, you'll inevitably hear someone sigh in their lawn chair and say, "Well, it might could be fixed if we just got the right Mayor."

And somewhere deep down by the creek, underneath a massive old tupelo tree, you can still find Boon on warm summer nights, those blue eyes glowing faintly in the moonlight, dropping ripe raspberries into the dark water, waiting for the big ones to bite. Because some folks are born to plow fields. Some folks are born to run for public office. And some folks, God bless 'em, are just born to feed the fat, sling a little mud, and keep this crazy world interesting.

CHAPTER TWENTY-FIVE:

THE GOSPEL OF "HEY, WATCH THIS"

Welcome to the absolute heart of Poo-Dunk County, Georgia—a place where the local speed limit is strictly defined as whatever maximum velocity your riding lawnmower or pickup truck can physically handle. You ain't gonna find no fancy streetlights or traffic enforcement 'round here; just the permanent smell of fresh-cut bahia grass and a whole lot of questionable personal decisions.

The undisputed kings of this county are two fellers named Boon and Earl Ray. Now, these two have witnessed more bizarre things in their lives than most folks have fingers and toes. They know the sacred, holy truth that when someone in Poo-Dunk yells, "Hey y'all, watch this!", your only sane move is to immediately take three steps back and grab a camera, 'cause things are about to get really interesting.

The boys are true artists of the broken, the busted, and the almost-useful. They can successfully repair anything equipped with a pulley or a pivot using nothing more than silver duct tape, chewing gum, wire coat hangers, and empty aluminum beer cans. They ain't just fixers, though; they're verified inventors! They regularly dream up contraptions that are plain redneck genius.

Take, for example, Earl Ray's patent-pending, portable, bank-fishing beer holder. It's nothing but a recycled beer can welded onto a piece of construction rebar and jabbed straight into the muddy riverbank—perfect for keeping your lukewarm brew stable beside you while you wait for a bite. Or that time Boon took a busted, oversized tractor tire, slapped a rubber plug into the sidewall hole, and turned it into a repurposed hillbilly bathtub out by the creek. They live fully for those moments that make a crowd go, "Looky there!" and, of course, the ever-famous emergency warning, "Hold my beer while I do this!"

The only thing more unpredictable than a July thunderstorm in this county is what Boon and Earl Ray are gonna come up with next. Bless their hearts, they save absolutely everything—rusty washing machines, old porcelain sinks, broken-down trucks, and cracked toilets. A man never knows when he will suddenly want to use an old plumbing fixture to complete a mechanical repair or decorate his front yard.

Of course, the local pet pigs make the absolute best mud bogs on the property. This year, the boys are throwing a neighborhood party to remember. Yup, twenty-five separate outdoor cookers will be frying everything imaginable: corn dogs, hush puppies (to shut up the barking yard dogs), chicken, okra, and plenty of ice-cold beer.

Tonight, the heat was thick and heavy, but the evening air was electric with the promise of beautiful chaos. The legendary "Beer Moon" was out, casting a pale, lunatic glow over Poo-Dunk, and everybody knew that when that specific moon rose above the pines, the local crazies came out with it.

Lying scattered across the cracked asphalt of the old feed store parking lot were three hundred bottle rockets—enough heavy artillery to launch a small-scale military invasion of a swamp. That was just the starting lineup. You also had a massive box of Black Cat firecrackers, a pile of Roman Candles the size of baseball bats, and a brick of industrial M80s.

Most of the older guys, like Boon and Earl Ray, had already learned their lessons the hard way over the decades. They knew that sooner or later, someone—usually some young buck trying desperately to impress a girl or just plain too drunk to remember last year's agonizing trip to the Emergency Room—was going to try something completely crazy.

"You remember Billy-Joe?" Boon asked, leaning his weight against his patched-up Ford, taking a long pull from a warm can. "Tried to light that entire string of firecrackers directly off his metal belt buckle. Ended up lookin' like a charcoal briquette in denim overalls."

Earl Ray chuckled, wiping his mouth with the back of his hand. "Naw, I'm thinkin' 'bout Skeeter Billy. Said lighting a bottle rocket out of his teeth was 'cooler than a corn dog at a county fair.' Found him an hour later sitting waist-deep in the creek trying to cool those facial burns."

But the night was still young, the master cooler was only half-empty, and over by the blazing bonfire, a skinny nineteen-year-old kid named Travis was already loudly proclaiming to the crowd, "Hey, watch this, y'all! I bet I can make this Roman Candle shoot twice as far if I hold the stick directly in my mouth!"

Boon and Earl Ray exchanged that classic, knowing look.

"Here we go again," Boon said, without wasting a single breath.

These young-uns don't even bother yelling "Hold my beer!" anymore. That specific phrase was officially retired in Poo-Dunk after the infamous Great Roman Candle Rodeo of '22. The two older men took two deliberate steps back into the shadows, cracked open fresh cold ones, and prepared their standard trauma kit: silver duct tape, chewing gum, a roll of paper towels, and a giant tub of industrial burn ointment.

It was the night before the Fourth of July, and that fat, hazy Beer Moon was hanging low over the river bottom—that special kind of summer moon that makes grown men do highly stupid things with black powder explosives. Three hundred bottle rockets, two gross of firecrackers, mortars, Roman candles, and one highly suspicious cardboard box labeled MYSTERY ASSORTMENT (PROBABLY LEGAL) sat piled high on the tailgate of Earl Ray's truck.

While Uncle Skeeter still couldn't feel three fingers on his left hand and Dale only possessed one working eyebrow from previous holidays, the young bucks were fresh, dumb, and full of clear moonshine and bad ideas.

"Bet you twenty bucks somebody sticks a live one in their butt crack before midnight," Boon muttered.

Earl Ray didn't even blink. "Make it fifty. I got immense faith in our local youth."

It didn't take long. Little Ricky—nineteen years old, completely shirtless, and wearing dark sunglasses at night—decided he was going to officially invent the "Bottle Rocket Boogie." He dropped his trousers right in the dirt, bent over like he was about to launch a NASA space shuttle, and wedged a lit bottle rocket firmly between his bare cheeks.

The fuse hissed angrily as the boys cheered him on. Boon and Earl Ray slowly shook their heads like disappointed fathers.

FWOOOOOSH!

Little Ricky shot across the dirt clearing like a human missile, screaming at the top of his lungs the entire way with his pants bound around his ankles, leaving a blinding trail of sparks behind him. He hit the creek bank at full speed, launched completely off the edge, and landed butt-first into three feet of muddy water with a massive splash that sounded like a Holstein cow hitting solid concrete.

For three glorious seconds, the entire clearing was completely quiet. Then the real screaming started.

Turns out the rocket motor hadn't actually gone out in the water; it was still fizzing and popping angrily in anatomical places no firework should ever go. Ricky came charging out of that creek doing the wildest, fastest version of the country hoedown the county had ever witnessed. He was slapping frantically at his own rear end like he thoroughly enjoyed being spanked.

Earl Ray let out a heavy sigh, took a long pull of his beer, and handed Boon a fresh roll of duct tape along with a fifty-dollar bill. "He's gonna need a tub of burn cream, a traveling priest, and probably a brand-new corporate butthole."

By the time 1 a.m. rolled around, the fireworks show had officially moved entirely from the sky to the ground. Somebody lit off a heavy mortar sideways into the lawn chairs. Another local genius attempted to juggle five lit Roman candles simultaneously. One fella even tried to literally "ride" a spinning wheel firework like a mechanical bull until the centrifugal force launched him directly into a heavy briar patch.

Boon and Earl Ray sat calmly on the truck tailgate the entire night like seasoned war veterans; they possessed the literal scars from doing the exact same things when they were teenagers. They sat comfortably handing out medical advice, duct-taping bleeding wounds, and offering lukewarm moral judgment with every fresh beer they opened.

Around 2 a.m., Little Ricky limped back over to the tailgate, walking exactly like a man who'd been horseback riding across the desert for three weeks straight without a saddle. His left butt cheek featured a perfectly symmetrical, rocket-shaped burn mark.

"Worth it," Ricky croaked, wincing as he sat on a cooler lid. "I think Sally-May saw me do it."

Boon looked at Earl Ray. Earl Ray looked at Boon. They both said at the exact same time: "Next year we're just buying sparklers and hand grenades."

Then they cracked open two more beers and immediately started taking cash bets on what dumbass things the town would come up with on New Year's Eve. Because in Poo-Dunk County, the Beer Moon always comes out, and so do the local idiots who are highly entertaining to watch.

A Note on Giving Back

In honor of the themes of hope, healing, and resilience woven throughout this story, a portion of the proceeds from the sale of this book will be proudly donated to St. Jude Children's Research Hospital. Thank you for your support with this book, which in turn helps support their vital mission of finding cures and saving children.

To my readers, thank you for stepping into the shadows of Peckville. I hope the story of Hunter, Spud, and Jim stays with you long after the final page is turned.

Made in the USA
Coppell, TX
15 July 2026

84148086R00103